CRAVING HIS COMMAND

CRAVING HIS COMMAND

A Doms of Genesis Novella

Jenna Jacob

Craving His Command
A Doms of Genesis Novella
Jenna Jacob

Published by Jenna Jacob
Copyright © 2017 Dream Words, LLC
Print Edition
Edited by: Blue Otter Editing, LLC
ISBN 978-0-9982284-6-4

This is a work of fiction. Names, places, characters and incidents are the product of the author's imagination and are fictitious. Any resemblance to actual persons, living or dead, events or establishments is solely coincidental.

To
Sean

CHAPTER ONE

Unable to find a comfortable position on the wooden bench outside the courtroom, Mercy O'Connor shifted her hips. She wouldn't be comfortable until this nightmare was over. The wait was driving her crazy.

This whole mess started three months ago. Davis Walker, a.k.a. Master Kerr, hadn't stopped when she'd screamed her safe word and beat her ass bloody during a BDSM scene gone wrong.

Forty-five minutes ago, Mercy had bravely taken the stand, ignoring Kerr's intimidating glare, and focused on answering the questions her lawyer, Reed Landes, asked. After Jeremy Potts, Kerr's lawyer, finished his cross-examination—hideously twisting her words—Reed did his best to deflect the damage done. Mercy wasn't holding her breath. Her hopes of winning the case had flown out the window when Potts painted her as a kinky, perverted freak instead of the victim. She'd wanted to vomit long before she left the stand shaking with fury. Mercy had bolted from the courtroom and escaped to the ladies' room to gather her wits and calm the hell down. But Kerr's demented gaze still stained her brain.

She knew she'd have to face the abusive prick when the verdict was read. Still, she couldn't find the courage to step inside the courtroom again, so she'd parked her ass on the unforgiving bench and waited to be summoned.

The nervous energy humming inside her threatened to burst free. Mercy rubbed her sweaty palms together and stood. As she paced, the heels of her black-bowed Miu Miu pumps clacked against the marble floor, echoing down the empty hallway like a cap gun.

The door behind her creaked. Mercy spun to find Reed Landes storming toward her. His expression, furious and grim.

"What happ—"

The question stalled on her tongue as Kerr sauntered into the hallway wearing a smarmy, triumphant grin.

The knots in her stomach coiled tighter. She didn't need a psychic to confirm that her efforts to bring Davis Walker to justice had failed. The look on his face was proof enough. Obviously the judge hadn't paid attention as Reed outlined the difference between consensual and non-consensual submission and Dominant ethics versus abusive predatory behavior. That, or maybe His Honor was so repulsed by the lifestyle he decided Mercy had simply gotten what she deserved.

Dammit!

Kerr turned his cold, maniacal grin her way. "Well, that didn't take long. I still have time to make the afternoon munch and share the news about my victory. Should I save you a seat, *Symoné?*"

Bile rose in the back of her throat when he referred to her as Symoné—the submissive name he'd given her years ago. Kerr's assumption that she'd go around the block with him filled her with a white-hot rage. The manipulative prick might have fooled her once, but she refused to be stupid enough to fall for his guise again. He could try and lure her in that low, inveigling whisper—that once had turned her on—until he was blue in face. She was learning the true meaning of submission since joining Club Genesis, and it was nothing close to what he'd led her to believe.

Mercy's stomach curdled as memories of surrendering to Kerr rushed in her head. Intimate, embarrassing visuals flashed like a repulsive slideshow…images of her *willingly* kneeling at the asshole's feet…worshiping his cock with her mouth as he fucked her throat. She could still hear his threats of reprisal if she failed to swallow all of his seed. Remembered him thrusting his pathetic cock inside her pussy and ass. Mercy wanted to bleach every humiliating moment that she'd allowed him to debase her from her memory banks. But she wanted to assuage the self-inflicted anguish and shame for letting him to play her like a damn puppet.

She'd spent the first half of her twenties fascinated by the BDSM lifestyle. Three years ago, after stumbling onto a website geared toward Doms and subs, Kerr friended her. After talking online for weeks, he'd offered to train her. Mercy had been thrilled that a real-life Master was willing to sate her curiosity and teach her to be a submissive. Hindsight being what it was, she'd been ridiculously naïve and so damn gullible.

Kerr had been convincing, she'd give him that, but his manufactured rules of the lifestyle and control he demanded she hand over had cost her dearly.

The memories continued to spill inside her brain like acid.

Kneel and open your mouth, slut. Prove you're a sub.

So she had.

You don't have any limits except the ones I give you. Our sessions aren't over until I decide it.

She hadn't opposed.

You'll take my cock up your ass because it's your duty to make me happy, whore.

She'd let him.

You're my property. I'll do whatever I want to you, and you'll fucking thank me when I'm through.

She hadn't protested.

You'll never find a better Master than me.

She'd believed him.

If you can't follow my commands, I'll find a sub who will.

She hadn't wanted to fail.

Kerr had brainwashed her into believing he was the only Master who'd provide her with the ultimate reward: submission. But it wasn't submission; it was abuse.

Mercy had been foolish and trusting. A mistake she wouldn't make again.

Her perception of submissive splendor now lay tarnished and stained in regret.

Humiliation and shame stung the backs of her eyes. She swallowed the greasy lump of guilt lodged in her throat and clenched her teeth. She refused to give Kerr the satisfaction of watching her fall apart.

"What do you say, *Symoné*...wanna hit the munch with me?"

Once upon a time, she'd looked forward to the weekly social outing where members of the BDSM community—well, Kerr's online recruits—gathered and discussed the lifestyle over lunch. To her delight, Club Genesis held munches as well, though work and preparing for the trial had prevented her from attending them yet.

She flashed Kerr a brittle smile. "There are no more munches. You're the only one left of our group because you ran everyone off with that stupid stunt you pulled on me in your so-called *dungeon*."

"Oh, I've made *new* friends…friends who know what real submission's about. Come on…I'll introduce you. It'll be just like old times."

The thought of Kerr luring more innocent subs to the slaughter filled her with dread. But overriding everything and scaring her senseless was the icy tone of retribution in Kerr's voice. In the past, Mercy thought him a demanding and strict Dom, but the night he'd lost his shit and unleashed his dark side had changed her opinion.

She was terrified of him. If Kerr ever got her alone, Mercy knew the authorities would never find her body.

An icy tremor slid up her spine.

"Why don't you do society a favor and crawl back under the rock you climbed out of, Kerr?" Reed sneered.

"Counselor!" Jeremy Potts—the sixty-something defense attorney, sporting a bad comb-over—admonished with a scowl. He clapped a protective hand on Kerr's shoulder. "Stooping to browbeat my client, now, are you? I didn't take you as the sore loser type, Landes."

"I didn't take you as the type to champion the scum-sucking dredges of the earth, either," Reed countered. "You that hard up for clients these days, Potts?"

The defense attorney's face grew crimson. The roadmap of broken capillaries on his nose and cheeks—suggesting a serious alcohol addiction—turned a mottled purple color. His nostrils flared and his bloodshot eyes narrowed in fury.

Mercy gaped at Reed, wondering where the kind and understanding lawyer she admired and trusted had gone. His usual mild manners had morphed and he'd turned into a battle-ready warrior, armed with a tongue honed like a blade and a take-no-prisoners attitude.

"Let's go, Davis. Our work here is done." Potts kept a seething glare locked on Reed as he gently nudged Kerr toward the elevator. "Until we meet again, Counselor."

It wasn't until the two were out of sight that Reed's palpable anger began to diminish.

"Kerr and his lawyer are a couple of peaches, aren't they?" Mercy drawled sarcastically.

"They're pieces of…work, that's for sure."

"I take it the judge had zero compassion for a woman who willingly allowed herself be cuffed to a cross and beaten?"

Reed's lips thinned to a tight line. "Campbell's a cantankerous old fuck. I knew when the original judge had to recuse himself and we drew Campbell, we were in for an uphill battle."

"*Original* judge? What do you mean?"

"Judge Graham was first slated to hear your case, but he knew Kerr…conflict of interest. So Graham declined and the clerk assigned Campbell."

"Ah, I see. So…that's it? It's over?"

"I'm afraid so." Reed frowned. "I'm sorry I wasn't able to give you the reparation you deserve."

Mercy shrugged absently. "You warned me from the start this would be a long shot. I'm just thankful that you tried."

Reed nodded dolefully. "I doubt Davis Walker will bother you, but hang on to the restraining order I filed, just in case."

"It's right here." She patted her purse and put on a brave face. "Don't worry. Kerr's nothing but a bully. I won't get close enough to the creep for him to hurt me again. I have a mean right hook I'm not afraid to use on him now."

"Let's hope it doesn't come to that. Would you like for me to walk you to your car?"

"No. Actually, mine's in the shop. My friend Maple dropped me off. I'm supposed to text her when I'm done and she'll pick me up. It's all good."

"Okay. I need to head down the hall. I've got another case in about twenty minutes."

"Thanks for *trying*, Reed, but mostly, thank you for not judging me or the lifestyle the way Campbell did."

"You're welcome, Mercy. I've never…I mean, I don't have any personal experience with…ah…" A light blush stained his cheeks as he stammered uncomfortably. "You're welcome."

Mercy bit back a grin. "Good luck with your next case."

"Thanks."

As Reed turned and walked away, she descended the stairs to the first floor, where she sent off a text to Maple. Before stepping outside, Mercy darted a glance both inside the lobby and over the courthouse grounds. Kerr was nowhere to be seen. But then, he had a lunch date with *new* potential victims. Mercy was certain the prick would garner a butt-load of sympathy because some crazy sub tried to send him to jail.

She slung her scarf around her neck and tugged the collar of her coat together before she pushed past the heavy glass door. A blustery November wind blew off Lake Michigan, sending brittle leaves of red, russet, and golden yellow to swirl at her feet. The wind bit her cheeks, and she was thankful she'd worn the brushed wool pants of her Dolce suit, instead of the skirt.

Peering up the street, she watched for Maple's red, sun-bleached Hyundai hatchback while business professionals hurried along the sidewalks, hunched over like trolls, shielding themselves from the cutting wind.

Still discouraged the court case was over, Mercy was also relieved. She could focus on work once more. She'd wasted her creative juices stressing about the trial and only managed to design one new logo for an existing nouveau-rich client. Now that all the ugliness was behind her, Mercy could concentrate on building her client base during the day and learning about *real* submission at night in the dungeon of Genesis.

"You're going to pay for humiliating me, bitch…pay a real high price."

Mercy snapped her head toward the savage sound of Kerr's unmistakable voice. He was standing a mere foot away from her. A ruthless rage blazed in his eyes, sending raw panic to unwind inside her. His crazed expression promised zero remorse if he slit her throat then and there.

Fear swelled to panic.

"You didn't actually think you'd get away with ruining my reputation, did you, cunt?"

Too petrified to respond, Mercy glanced at the strangers traversing the sidewalk. The bevy of bodies were only a few yards away, they might as well have been miles. If Kerr whipped out a knife or a gun, she'd be dead before anyone could reach her…*if* they bothered to intervene at all.

Mercy thought of the restraining order in her purse, but a piece of paper was useless in a face-to-face confrontation like this. Besides, there wasn't a cop in sight to enforce the damn thing.

She was on her own.

With her options limited, she did the only thing she could think of…she turned and ran.

Kerr's demonic laughter followed her on the wind as she sprinted up the stairs and bolted inside the courthouse. When she skidded to a stop, the two security guards manning the metal detectors snapped their concerned looks her way. Mercy's heart sank. She hadn't noticed the men were old as dirt, frail, and as intimidating as newborn kittens on her first trip through the checkpoint. A stiff wind could knock the old farts down. Combined, the pair couldn't provide the level of resistance needed to stop Kerr.

As she watched her purse inch along the conveyer belt and through the x-ray machine, her fear continued to climb. She darted a sidelong glance toward the entrance and spied Kerr walking with a lackadaisical stride toward the building. Pinning one more hopeless look on the guards, Mercy could all but see the pair fumbling for their guns while Kerr gripped her by the hair and dragged her away.

No, she wasn't putting her life in the hands of two potentially inept men.

Her hammering heart echoed in her ears as she grabbed her purse and raced up the stairs. The second floor yawed in front of her. Mercy pushed off the balls of her feet, clamoring to reach the landing and find Reed.

Once at the top, she made a beeline for Campbell's courtroom. Maybe if the judgmental dipshit saw Kerr in action, he might rethink his decision to let the monster go free. She pulled back on the door handle only to find it locked.

Adrenaline thundered through her bloodstream, making her limbs tingle as she ran to the next door. That courtroom was locked as well.

"Oh, come on!" she growled as she sprinted to the next portal.

"Symoné!" Kerr's voice—a sickening singsong tenor—taunted from the stairwell. Each thud of his shoes echoing on the steps felt as if he were stomping the air from her lungs. "Where are you? I'm coming…"

The prick was playing a demented game of cat and mouse. If she didn't find help, fast, she'd face the unimaginable—torture and a slow, suffering death.

Shaking uncontrollably, she bit back a sob of terror. Mercy sent up a silent prayer as she gripped the door handle and tugged. The slab of polished oak careened open, and she yelped in surprise as she skimmed a quick glance over the empty courtroom. She was grateful to find a safe haven, at least until she saw the brass plaque atop the magistrate's perch:

JUDGE KELLAN GRAHAM.

Judge Graham was first slated to hear your case, but he knew Davis Walker…conflict of interest… Reed Landes' words tumbled through her head as dread rolled up her spine.

"Oh, god," Mercy whimpered. "Of all the lousy luck."

Thankfully, Kerr's judge *friend* was long gone. But his courtroom was not the safe haven she'd first thought. Hopefully, Murphy's Law wouldn't bring his gavel down, and she could hide here undetected by Judge Kellan Graham until Kerr had abandoned his search of the second floor and moved onto the third. Then she could haul her ass home.

Gripping both handles of the door, Mercy pressed her forehead to the wood. She closed her eyes and listened. The echo of Kerr's footsteps grew closer. Enveloped in a feeling of helplessness, Mercy wanted to scream at the madman to go away. Instead, she pinched her lips together as tears spilled down her cheeks. Strangled sobs burned the back of her throat. Squeezing the handles tighter, Mercy wasn't giving up. She'd go down screaming, fighting, kicking, and biting if she had to.

Call Reed.

Call the police…the fucking National Guard…for shit's sake, call someone! her subconscious screamed.

But Mercy couldn't risk taking her hands off the door to retrieve her phone from her purse. She lifted her head and spied a silver deadbolt shimmering above her hands.

Visions of Kerr crashing through the portal before she could engage the lock pelted her psyche, but Mercy refused to cower to him or her fears. Sucking in a deep breath, she flipped the latch with trembling fingers. The snick of the lock sent relief to storm her system. Though she was far from being out of danger, the temporary reprieve filled her with hope. Hope that Kerr might think she'd taken refuge in another room and move on so she could run away from this labyrinth of fear.

Interminable anxious seconds slowly ticked by while sweat and tears slid down her face.

Suddenly, with what felt like the force of an earthquake, the door shook.

Mercy slapped a hand over her mouth to hold back a scream while a little voice inside her head beckoned her to *run!*

Blinded by a frenzy of fear, she turned and slammed into a wide black wall that nearly knocked the wind out of her. Strong masculine arms gripped her shoulders.

"Whoa." A deep, whiskey-smooth voice vibrated through her. "Do you need help, miss?"

Mercy didn't answer. The debilitating terror coursing through her veins had rendered her mute. As she fought to suck air into her lungs, she realized something else was chasing the cyclone of panic racing through her. The stranger's touch had ignited an arc of heat that tingled down her limbs, up her spine, and gathered between her legs. Bewildering carnal sparks tangled with terror and sputtered through her. She tried to pass off the sensation as part of the enormous adrenaline dump that was taking place inside her, but deep down, she knew the familiar ache was wholly sexual. Confused by the untimely awakening in her panties, Mercy tried to sort the barrage of conflicted emotions as she stared at the crisp pressed pleats of black fabric in front of her face. When she was finally able to gather enough courage, she raised her chin and gasped.

A shudder tore through her as she gazed into the familiar sapphire eyes of Sir Justice. The allusive and intriguing Dom from Club Genesis who'd captured her attention and invaded her dreams for the past three months. For a moment, Mercy wondered if this were simply another frustrating dream. But as she watched a parade of emotions march across his face, she knew this wasn't another one of her sexually charged fantasies.

"Symoné?" He whispered her name. It felt like a caress.

Tongue-tied, Mercy couldn't respond. She simply stared, slack-jawed, at the mysterious Dom. Up close and personal with him now, his commanding aura made her want to fall at his feet and satisfy him in every way, even more. He'd watched her for months from across the dungeon...dissecting her every move, and made her wish for things she probably wasn't ready to handle...*him*!

But Mercy feared her attraction to Sir Justice, a.k.a. Judge Kellan Graham, was one-sided. Not once had he ever approached her...never even spoken to her. Yet every time she laid eyes on the man, her heart rate quickened and her panties flooded—like they were doing now. But that didn't keep her from fantasizing about him. Each time she pulled the toys from her bedside table, he was there with her—in her mind and in her body—sinking deep inside her slippery pussy until she shattered beneath his imaginary touch.

Unable to find her voice, Mercy stared at the sculpted planes of his handsome face…studied the texture of his full, inviting lips.

He was dangerously sexy.

Demand streaked through her like a meteorite crashing to earth.

Her pussy plumped.

Her tunnel clutched.

Her clit pulsed with an intoxicating throb.

But when the door violently rattled again, the sublime sexual thoughts consuming her instantly turned to panic. Mercy snapped her head toward the sound as she tried to wriggle from the grasp of her fantasy Dom. But Justice simply held on tighter.

This was it.

The end.

Judge Kellan Graham, a.k.a. Sir Justice, was going to offer her up, like a sacrificial lamb, to his *friend* Kerr. Unable to process the overload of terror, Mercy's brain shut down.

The room began to swim.

The sexy Dom's face before her blurred and darkness closed in all around her.

W*HAT*. T*HE*. F*UCK*?

"No!" Kellan barked.

But even his harsh command couldn't keep the sinfully sexy sub from fainting.

He should have known when Symoné's face turned a ghostly shade of white the girl was going down. He'd been too shocked to find her in his courtroom, and so fucking mesmerized by her dazzling aqua-colored eyes—well, until they rolled to the back of her head—that he damn near hadn't caught her as she crumpled to the floor.

He held her soft, warm body in his arms, feeling as if he'd just taken a lightning bolt to the chest. Any second now, he'd spontaneously combust.

"Shit!"

The door rattled once more.

Ignoring the distraction, Kellan hoisted Symoné's unconscious body into his arms. Even before he'd touched her, he'd been humming in arousal, but now…he was boiling.

As he settled her against his chest, her purse slid off her shoulder and caught at the bend of her elbow. The bag swung in a wide arc and caught him square in the nuts. With a grunt, Kellan froze and sucked in a quick breath. Holding the air in his lungs, he cringed and waited for pain to twist his gut. He didn't have to wait long. Air exploded from his lips, and he croaked out a curse. Clutching Symoné tight to his chest, Kellan doubled over.

What the fuck is she carrying in that purse…bricks?

Pain clawed through him. Kellan closed his eyes and tried to breathe as agony assaulted his balls, but his focus was ambushed with questions.

What was Symoné doing in his courtroom, and why was she so frightened?

Suddenly the puzzle pieces aligned.

Kerr.

Memories of the night Symoné came crashing into Kellan's controlled and disciplined world, like a goddamn wrecking ball, flashed in his mind.

It had started several months ago when Mika LaBrache, Owner of the BDSM Club Genesis, revoked Kerr's contract and banned the asswipe for ignoring a sub's safe word. Kellan and several other Doms received the honor of physically tossing Kerr's ass to the curb. It was one of the best nights Kellan had ever had in the club.

A few weeks later, Kerr called and invited Kellan to join the wannabe Dom's new dungeon he'd opened named Control.

When Kellan informed Mika of Kerr's unwanted solicitation, shit went south, fast. Four members of Genesis infiltrated Club Control—or rather the seedy loft with shoddy play equipment—under the guise of wanting a new dungeon to call home. In reality, the four had gone to Kerr's club to warn unsuspecting subs about his abusive reputation in the kink community. The prick had cuffed Symoné to the cross and proceeded to demonstrate his *Dominant prowess* by tearing the poor girl's ass up with a leather paddle. When she began screaming her safe word, Kerr refused to relent. The four visitors, Max, Dylan, Nick, and

Savannah, stepped in. They brought Symoné—who'd bravely filed assault charges against Kerr—and seven other subs back to Genesis that night.

Kellan stared at the limp sub in his arms.

"Today's the hearing. That's why you're here, isn't it?" he asked the still-unconscious woman.

She had to be hiding from Kerr.

Kellan glanced over his shoulder. Though moments ago he'd dismissed the rattling door, he suspected Kerr had been stalking her and attempting to change the outcome of his fate through intimidation. Kellan's emotions were divided. He refused to leave Symoné passed out and alone, but he desperately wanted to satisfy his curiosity. If Kerr was out there, Kellan was ready to beat the ever-living fuck out of him.

Still recovering from the shot to his crotch, Kellan slowly stood and stared down at the alluring woman in his arms. Drinking in her the soft contours of her face, he locked onto the lush bow of her lips. He ached to press his mouth to hers…listen to her purr as he surged inside and explored every nook and cranny…feast on the woman who'd haunted his dreams for three long, frustrating months.

He'd spent too many years denying himself pleasure.

No matter how hard he tried—and he'd tried mightily—Kellan couldn't purge her from his system. Symoné possessed some kind of magnetic pull over him. Her beauty enthralled him—even more so in his arms—resistance was futile. Slanting in close to her mouth, he felt her moist breath flutter against his lips. He dipped his head and closed his eyes.

What the fuck are you doing? Have you lost your damn mind? She's unconscious! This isn't consensual, asshole! Christ, why don't you just lay her on the ground, yank her pants off, and fuck her while you're at it.

At his conscience's scolding, Kellan jerked his head upright. Panic and irritation with himself made for an ugly cocktail. Even when she was passed out, he couldn't resist the minx. He felt like she was trying to steal his soul, test his resolve, and rattle his control. Kellan had to be stronger, or he'd fold like a deck of cards. There was too much at stake for him to lose his fucking spine. Ever since he'd laid eyes on the sassy sub, she'd starting challenging his orderly world.

Symoné was a complication he didn't need. He was struggling enough.

"It doesn't matter," he muttered. He couldn't touch her the way he longed to, not now...not ever.

A tremor of frustration rippled through him.

Biting back a curse, he carried her to his private chambers and grudgingly laid her on the leather loveseat near his desk. His arms felt strangely empty, but Kellan dismissed the absurdity of what that meant and retrieved a bottle of water from the mini-fridge on the other side of the room.

Symoné was still unconscious as he knelt beside her. Brushing a few errant strands of hair from her face, Kellan stared at her long, dark lashes resting against her porcelain flesh. Tears of terror stained her cheeks, making him want to find Kerr and break his skinny little neck once more. There'd be time later to deal with the douchebag. Right now this precious sub needed his help.

"Symoné. It's time to wake up, angel," he whispered.

Her plump, kissable lips taunted him, making his pulse race. Reaching out, he wanted to caress her face...lean in and kiss her awake, but he quickly pulled his hand away. If he touched her now, he'd never find the willpower to stop until he was balls deep inside her. Annoyed with his surging testosterone, he clenched his jaw. The sooner she woke up, the sooner he could escort her to her car and salvage his precarious control.

"Come on, Symoné. You need to wake up."

She didn't respond. Kellan began to worry that he'd have to call the EMTs and have her taken to the hospital.

No way! If anyone's taking her to a hospital, it'll be me!

"Symoné!" With a firm voice, he gently shook her shoulder.

A tiny moan slid off her lips as her eyelids fluttered open.

"There you are. Welcome back." He forced a smile, hoping to reassure her and erase the confusion from her face.

"Sir Justice? What are you...Where am I?"

"You were hiding out in my courtroom, but you're in my chambers now, safe and sound." He hadn't meant for his voice to sound so gruff and cold.

Symoné wrinkled her brow and lowered her lids, but not before he saw rejection and sadness fill her eyes. He inwardly cursed himself for being such an ass. Biting his tongue to keep from upsetting her more, Kellan twisted the cap from the water bottle. He cupped the back of her neck and raised her head before placing the rim to her lips. When she wrapped her mouth around the bottle, a ridiculous pang of envy punched his gut. She tilted her chin when she'd had enough, the way the subs at Genesis often did while riding the clouds of endorphins. A potent rush of Dominance charged through him. Kellan wanted nothing more than to command this glorious sub's pleasure and pain until the end of time.

Focus, fucker!

"Are you feeling better?"

Symoné nodded. "Yes, thank you. You're Judge Graham, right?"

"I am."

"Now I understand why you couldn't hear my case."

"Reed told you about that, did he?"

Her nape was singeing his fucking palm making it hard as hell to carry on a polite conversation.

Again she nodded and turned a nervous glance toward the door. "Is Kerr still out there looking for me?"

"I don't know. While you were passed out, I put two and two together. I didn't want to leave you alone and go off hunting for the prick."

When he tipped the bottle to her lips again, she reached up with trembling hands and gripped the plastic. Kellan stood and stepped back. He watched her throat work as she swallowed the liquid, wishing instead of water she was guzzling down the seed churning in his balls.

"What time is your hearing?" he asked. His voice came out raspy and low.

"It's…over," she murmured. A grim expression lined her lips as she set the water on the floor. "Kerr's foot loose and free. I lost."

"You mean Reed just walked away and left you to deal Kerr on your own?" Kellan could feel his blood pressure spiking.

"No. He offered to walk me to my… Oh, crap." Her eyes grew wide she and sat upright, wobbling slightly.

"Easy. What's wrong?"

"I need my purse. I have to call Maple. She was coming to pick me up. Ugh. She's probably outside driving around the building, pissed or worried that I haven't come out yet."

Kellan plucked her combination leathal weapon and designer purse off the floor and placed it in her lap. After wiggling out of her coat,

Symoné plucked out the device, looked at the screen, and groaned.

Kellan didn't want to imagine her making that same sound beneath him in a big, soft bed...but he did.

"Is there a problem?"

"Yes...no." She shook her head. "Maple's car has a flat and she's waiting for Triple A."

"Text her back and tell her you have a ride home." Though his tone wasn't as icy this time, he'd inadvertently pulled out his unrelenting Dom voice. But then, if the shoe fit...

"I do?"

"Yes. I'm taking you home." *Unfortunately, not home with me. Dammit.*

"You can't," she protested. Kellan arched his brows and leveled Symoné with a hard stare. "I-I mean...it's...I-I'm sure it's out of your way. I won't inconvenience you like that, Sir. I'll call Uber or catch a cab."

"You'll do nothing of the kind. I'm taking you home and that's final. Kerr might still be prowling the courthouse. I wont risk him finding you. God only knows what he plans to put you through next."

"He wants to kill me." She blurted out the words as the color drained from her face.

"Excuse me?"

"He told me I wasn't going to get away with humiliating him, and trust me, if looks could kill, I'd be dead already."

Her voice quivered and Kellan's heart tripped double time. An internal possessive roar filled his ears.

"Exactly why I'm taking you home." He drew in a deep breath and slowly released it while tempering the urge to murder the bastard. "I don't care how far out of the way it might be, I want you safe, Sym...What is your real name?"

A light blush painted her cheeks as she stretched out her hand. "It's Mercy...Mercy O'Connor."

He smiled and placed his hand in hers as a strange heat warmed his skin. The messy complications he'd been avoiding for months suddenly became even more real. Though he wasn't ready to admit it, Kellan knew he was fucked.

"Oh, my," she gasped.

Mercy's eyes grew wide. She tried to pull her hand back, but he simply held on tight. "It's a pleasure to meet you, Mercy O'Connor. I'm Kellan Graham, but you know that all ready."

Her shy smile and darkening blush kicked him in the gut, but he couldn't afford to let lust sidetrack him.

"Before we leave. I need to gather some papers from my bench. You go ahead and lie back and relax...sip some water, I won't be long."

Her compliant nod stroked his Dominance like a caress. Blood surged south as his cock lengthened and grew thick. He was glad as fuck his robe concealed his erection. Still, irritation chewed within. He flattened his lips and strode out the door.

Sitting at his bench, surrounded by the soothing familiarity, Kellan shuffled papers, waiting for his cock to deflate. Angry voices from the hallway grabbed his attention. He hurried across the room and flipped the lock before stepping out to find Judge Dupree looking as if he wanted to bring his gavel down on a stringy blond-haired man who was snarling and cursing. The vulgar-talking prick didn't even have to turn around. Kellan knew instantly it was Kerr.

"What are you still doing here, Walker?" Kellan asked.

Kerr spun around. His eyes grew wide before a cynical smile speared his lips. "So you're a judge? I'll be damned. *Justice* seems all the more fitting, now."

"Your trial was over long ago. You've got thirty seconds to get your ass out of the building and off government property, or I'll have you tossed in a cell," Kellan warned, looking at his watch. "Twenty-nine, twenty-eight."

"I'll tell you, like I told this idiot,"—Kerr pointed to Dupree—"I ain't leaving till I find someone."

"You're not going to *find* her. I've already made sure of that. Leave," Kellan barked. "Nineteen, eighteen..."

"You can't protect her forever."

"Is that a threat, Walker?" A nasty grin tugged Kellan's lips.

Kerr's face turned red as he darted a glance at Dupree. "No. But I *will* find her."

Before Kellan could issue another warning, the maggot turned and ran away.

"Friend of yours?" Dupree asked.

"No. A rodent who needs to be exterminated."

"I can't argue that."

Kellan nodded, doing the best he could to mask the rage boiling within as he turned and walked away. He bypassed the bench and stormed back into his office. Mercy was now sitting on the edge of the couch, sipping water. She turned her eyes up at him. Though Kellan wanted to get lost in her aqua pools, he strode to his desk, removed his robe, and draped it over his chair.

"Are you ready to leave?" he asked in a dispassionate tone.

"Yes, but I don't want to put you out. I'll catch a—"

"Dammit, Mercy." Kellan slammed his fist on his desk.

She jolted and curled in on herself. He pinched the bridge of his nose with his finger and thumb and sucked in a ragged breath.

"I'm sorry. I had no right to rip into you like that. Kerr's still here. I just had a conversation with him in the hall. He knows to leave or be arrested, but I don't trust the prick to heed my warning. So, I *am* taking you home, and that's the end of this discussion."

Even from across the room, Kellan saw the tremor of fear ripple through Mercy's body. "He won't rest until he's gotten his revenge, will he?"

Probably, but he wasn't going admit that and scare her even more.

"The man's warped. I'll do all I can to keep you safe. You have my word."

Mercy lowered her lashes and focused on the empty water bottle in her hand. "Thank you for your help, but I'll have to confront him eventually. I can't run and hide like a scared rabbit the rest of my life." Her barely audible tone lacked the conviction of her words.

"Does Walker know where you live?"

"Yes." She sighed heavily.

"Do you have a house or—"

"An apartment. I live at Elmhurst Lake in Highland Park."

Kellan was impressed. Even a one-bedroom apartment at the upscale complex cost an arm and a leg. But he was more taken aback by the fact that she lived so close to him. "I have a place in Highland Park, myself. In fact, I'm less than a mile down the beach from you. So, see? Taking you home isn't out of my way at all."

"Small world." She flashed him a smile that made him want to moan. "I guess 'howdy neighbor' is in order then."

"Howdy." He smirked, then turned sober. "Do you own a gun?"

"I'm from Texas. My Daddy taught me to shoot before I was old enough to drive."

Kellan knew she was trying to make light of the subject, but she couldn't erase the fear still swimming in her eyes. "What happened to Kerr? He wasn't like this before he got shot. I mean, he was always an ass, but he was never violent."

"I don't know. I do know he died that night on the dungeon floor before the EMTs brought him back to life. Maybe he suffered brain damage from lack of oxygen or something. Hard to say. I do know one thing…he's not going to give up, at least not today. The best we can hope is that he simply needs a little time to cool off."

"And lick his wounded pride," she added dolefully. "I'll be careful. Don't worry."

Not careful enough.

Kellan was two seconds from offering to put Mercy up in his guest room. If he wouldn't lie awake all night concocting reasons to sneak into her room, crawl into her bed, and fuck her to oblivion, he'd cart her straight home.

But a masochist he wasn't.

Besides, he had a vow to keep—one that didn't allow him to bed any sub.

Mercy isn't just any sub…not by a long shot.

CHAPTER TWO

KELLAN'S ENTICING, MASCULINE SCENT filled her senses and soaked her panties. Mercy was still working to wrap her head around the fact that the standoffish Dom was actually speaking to her. She felt as if she'd won the lottery ten times over. One thing was certain; talking to him was a hell of a lot more interesting than him simply watching her like he always did in the dungeon. At first Mercy had found it endearing that the handsome Dom took an interest in her. His dissecting stare only fueled her fantasies about him all the more. But night after night he never approached her. His scrutiny felt a bit creepy and downright intimidating. Still, his strange behavior didn't diminish her craving for him. The man was—a shiver rippled through her—delicious.

Gazing up at him, Mercy found herself biting back a grin. *Sir Justice* was an actual judge. She'd always assumed his club name was simply a metaphor designed to instill good behavior among the subs. His reputation at Genesis was that of a soft-spoken, gentle Master.

Mercy hadn't seen much of his fabled temperament so far. He seemed irritated, cranky, and on edge. She didn't know if Kerr, herself, or something else was to blame for Kellan's sour mood, but she certainly wasn't going to ask what had crawled up his butt. Instead, she cast her eyes to the floor. Not only was it the proper submissive thing to do but it also kept her from gawking at him like a lovesick puppy.

While she wished Kellan shared the same infatuation for her that she did him, his distance screamed he wasn't interested in Mercy *or* her submission. He was probably only speaking to her now because he was too much of a gentleman to leave her passed out on the courtroom floor for the cleaning crew to discover.

Suddenly, Kellan thrust his capable-looking fingers toward her. Mercy locked a startled gaze on him. "I-I'm sorry. Did you say something?"

"I asked if you were ready to leave." His frown deepened. "Are you sure you're all right?"

"I'm fine. Honest…just a bit freaked out."

It wasn't a lie. Kellan put her completely off-balance, but oh, how she craved him.

If she didn't fear him shooting her down like a pheasant, she'd wrap her arms around his neck and kiss him blind. But rejection would be crushing and mortifying. She inhaled a steely breath and slid her fingers into his palm. That familiar and crazy rush of heat enveloped her once again.

Her girl parts started throwing a throb party, like they'd done before she passed out.

"That's completely understandable," Kellan quietly agreed as he helped her to her feet. "But Kerr can only hold the power you give him."

"Yes, Sir, I know," she replied before sliding her coat on.

Heat flared in Kellan's eyes before he quickly banked it and clenched his jaw. Without another word, he plucked a large leather briefcase off the floor and led her out the door.

As they waited for the elevator, Kellan continuously swept his eyes over the hallway, searching for Kerr. An awkward tension hung in the air like a thick fog. When the elevator dinged, Mercy nearly jumped out of her skin.

Kellan sent her a sympathetic smile. "You're safe, angel."

Angel? His term or endearment made her knees weak. She felt small and fragile.

When the shiny metal doors opened, he placed a wide hand against the small of her back and ushered her inside. Heat spread up her spine and down her legs, making her skin tingle and burn. Sparks sputtered and popped inside her long after the doors closed and Kellan dropped his hand.

He stood ramrod straight, shoulders square, and chin slightly lifted. As he stared straight ahead, Mercy drank in every nuance of the man…from the sexy black scruff adorned with a few gray flecks lining his rugged jaw to his large hands and big feet. If the motto was true, then Kellan was hung like a damn horse.

A rush of heat blasted up her body.

He was several years older than her, a fact that added to the mystique of a mature and experienced man. He'd know his way around a woman's body...around *her* body.

As if you'll ever find out, the little voice in her head taunted.

The mixed emotions he evoked were maddening, but instead of attempting to sort them in the small descending cubicle, she continued to study him.

The slope of his nose was regal like a Greek God and his lips... Lord, she'd give anything to press her mouth to those kissable pillows for weeks...months...years.

A tiny smile kicked up the side of his face. "What are you staring at?" he asked without looking her way.

"You."

"Why?"

"Um, because..." *You're drop-dead gorgeous, and I'm dying to rip that conservative suit off your hot body, slam you up against the wall, and fuck your brains out.* "I've never seen you up close before. You're always hiding in the shadows of the dungeon, watching me."

Mercy issued an inward groan. Instead of calling him out for his furtive behavior at the club, she should have confessed about wanting to fuck him senseless.

His smile broadened as he turned and arched his brows at her. "How do you know I watch you?"

She rolled her eyes. "I'm not blind."

"Neither am I." His expression suddenly hardened. "How many Doms have asked you to scene with them since you joined Genesis?"

Mercy mentally scrambled to come up with a number. "I don't know. Eight or nine."

"Twelve," Kellan replied in a clipped and brittle tone.

The elevator doors opened and he strode away. For a stunned second, Mercy gaped at his retreating form before marching after him. Her heels clopped on the cement floor of the parking garage.

"You've kept track?"

"Yes."

"Why?"

Kellan didn't answer as he paused at a sleek, black BMW i8. When he touched the handle on the passenger side, the locks disengaged. He held the door open for her with an unreadable expression. "Get in."

Mercy had ached to heed his command for months, yet the first one he lobbed her way had made her hackles rise. "Not until you tell me why you've kept count of the Doms who've approached me."

"Get in so I can take you home, angel."

His low, inveigling tone contradicted his imposing glare. Clearly her ultimatum had crawled under his Dominant skin. She'd roused Sir Justice. His big, bad, bold command roared to life and that authoritative mien lit her up like a firecracker. Mentally cursing her gushing hormones, she fought the dizzying wave of demand that rolled from her toes all the way to her scalp.

A soft shiver racked her body as she slid onto the butter-soft leather passenger seat.

Pride prompted her to keep pushing him, but she knew going toe-to-toe with a Dom was a no-no. While Mercy wasn't privy to the finer intricacies of submission, she knew enough to back down, at least for now.

After he'd climbed in behind the wheel and maneuvered onto the busy street, Mercy turned his way. "What should I call you? Sir Justice or Kellan?"

"Outside the club, Kellan is fine. Inside, Sir will do nicely."

"Does that mean you actually plan to *speak* to me at the club?" She shot him a taunting smirk.

He scowled as an indecisive noise rumbled deep in his throat. "I'll think about it."

"What's there to think about?" she scoffed. "Is my past association with Kerr so disgraceful that I'm unworthy of a friendly hello from time to time?"

"Hell no! Kerr doesn't have shit to do with anything."

"Then what is it?"

"I have my reasons. They don't concern you."

"Obviously they do." She knew she should shut up, but she couldn't keep from poking and prodding. "You don't have a problem talking or scening with any of the other subs…just me. Why is that?"

"So…you've been watching me, too? Tell me something, why haven't *you* ever spoken to me?"

"You didn't answer my question."

"You've not answered mine, either."

I asked you first. The childish retort smoldered on the tip of her tongue. Mercy swallowed it down and lifted her chin. "Because I'm not supposed to."

"Says who?"

"Approaching a Dom is not proper submissive behavior."

"Who told you that?" Kellan's brows wrinkled.

Mercy dropped her eyes to her lap. She didn't want to confess it was one of Kerr's many stupid rules. Based on Kellan's reaction, she assumed it was another lie Davis Walker had spoon-fed to her to keep Mercy from seeking out other more qualified Doms.

"You don't need to answer, I already know…Kerr." Kellan exhaled in disgust. "I'm going to give you a piece of advice. Throw away everything that idiot taught you about the lifestyle and start attending the Saturday morning submissive classes at the club."

"I've been meaning to, but I've been too busy with the hearing and work."

"Find a way to free up some time. If you truly want to learn about the lifestyle, then you need to make the sub meetings a priority." He paused for several seconds. "What kind of work do you do?"

"I'm a freelance designer. Corporate branding, mostly."

"An artist, huh? You must be talented as hell to afford Elmhurst Lake."

She was surprised that Kellan knew her apartment complex charged a pretty penny for its units. The fact that Mercy paid more in rent than a lot of urban professionals did a house payment suddenly made her self-conscious. But what Kellan didn't know was that her company had taken off so quickly, she needed the tax write-off working from home provided. Besides, the killer view of Lake Michigan was well worth the extra money.

"Just lucky." She shrugged. "The right doors swung open when I first started my company. Word of mouth has kept me in toothpaste and corn flakes."

"Modest much?" He smirked. "Who are some of your clients?"

She shot him a suspicious glance. "Why do you want to know?"

"Your secrets are safe with me, angel."

His sexy voice cascaded down her flesh like whiskey poured over velvet. She couldn't keep from naming off her Fortune 500 clients anymore than she could fly out the sunroof.

Kellan arched his brows. "For such a young woman, you've

amassed an impressive list."

"I'm not that young, but thank you." She blushed.

The wide grin he flashed her way made Mercy's heart skip.

"I own socks that are older than you, girl."

When she laughed, Kellan's nostrils flared and he gripped the steering wheel tighter.

"You have twenty-eight-year-old socks? I don't believe that."

"You're only twenty-eight?"

"What do you mean *only*? I'm on the downhill slide to thirty."

"Oh, you poor baby," he chided dryly.

"How old are you?"

"Too old."

"Too old for what?" she asked in a surprisingly sultry tone.

She felt him tense from across the vehicle. He remained quiet, as if pondering her question. "Skateboarding."

She laughed again. "Me, too. I mean, honestly…who wants to break a hip?"

"That could easily happen to me," he chuckled. "I'm practically a dinosaur."

"Hardly," she said with a pfft sound. "You haven't grown scales or claws or big scary teeth yet."

"Yet," he repeated with a crooked smile. "I suspect any day now, I'll wake up, look in the mirror and…well, it won't be pleasant."

"I don't think you have anything to worry about for a couple million years or so."

The excitement inside her glittered. She'd finally cracked his impenetrable veneer. The man within had a dry but witty sense of humor. Mercy realized the prickly pins and needles that had been scraping her flesh earlier had disappeared.

Kellan was an enigma to be sure, but she hoped their playful verbal jousting might be the beginning of a more profound friendship. Of course, it might be nothing more than him chasing silence with nonsensical banter while navigating the congested highway.

"You said you were from Texas, but I detect a hint of something else in your accent."

"Like what?"

"Like Southern meets East Coast."

"You have a good ear, Judge. No one else has picked up the gypsy inside me."

"Moved around a lot, have you?"

"No, but I do love to travel. I grew up a couple hours northwest of Dallas on a ranch in the middle of nowhere. I'm talking *nowhere*. Our nearest neighbor was eighteen miles away. My dad is what you'd call a modern-day cattle baron. He raises and breeds longhorns, well, he and my brothers."

"How many brothers do you have?"

"Four, all older."

"I read an article about longhorns once. That can be a lucrative business."

"Thankfully for Dad it is. That's the only way I could have ever attended Cornell University. I studied there for a couple years, then transferred to the School of the Art Institute of Chicago."

"Was New York too much culture shock for you?"

"It wasn't so much the culture shock…" Mercy paused and weighed how much personal information she wanted to share. No one but family knew why she'd escaped the Big Apple, but for some unknown reason, she felt compelled to tell Kellan everything. "My roommate committed suicide, and I was the one who found her."

"Oh, angel." A pained expression lined his face. "I'm sorry. Did you know she had problems?"

"No." A fact that still filled her with guilt. "She was always the life of the party…happy…spontaneous."

"Are you sure it was a suicide?"

"Yes. She left a note. Her boyfriend had dumped her." Mercy's anger bubbled to the surface the way it always did when she thought of Mary Jo—the pretty girl from Nebraska with flaming-red hair, freckles, and a fucking heart of gold. "She offed herself over some asshole who didn't bother showing up for her funeral. I swear, taking your life because of some guy is a stupid and pathetic reason to check out, you know?"

Kellan sent her a nod. His eyes were brimmed in sadness, but he didn't try to stop her from baring her soul.

"I don't understand why Mary Jo gave that bastard the right to destroy her. We all screw up. I did when I gave Kerr the power to hurt me, but no man is worth swallowing a bottle of pills over. I'd never give anyone that much control over me…ever."

"You shouldn't."

She sent him a quizzical stare. "I didn't expect to hear that from the lips of a Dom."

"There's a big difference between a sub giving her power to a Dom and some asshole demanding she hand it over to him. That you already know."

"True. But I don't know where or when to draw the line? I mean...there's a part inside me that craves to hand over everything, but at the same time, I have no desire to lose my identity in the process. Submission is such a paradox to me. I was raised to be independent and headstrong, which I am...outside the club. Then there's another part of me that wants to wrap up the liberated, stubborn pieces of myself into a big ball and hand them to a worthy Dominant." A scowl wrinkled her forehead. "It sounds stupid now, but when I was with Kerr, I thought I'd found the elusive peace I'd been searching for."

"That's not stupid. I'm sure you achieved a level of subspace through all his bullshit. But trust me. There's a whole lot more out there waiting for you to experience."

"I BELIEVE YOU, but when I found out everything he'd led me to believe was a lie, I wanted to throw my dreams of submission away."

"Don't do that. You'll only be cutting off your nose to spite your face."

"I won't." Kellan watched her cheeks glow crimson. "Sorry about that. I don't know how I went from Mary Jo to submission."

"No. Don't ever apologize for asking questions or trying to sort your feelings," Kellan softly stated.

If he could take her under his Dominant wing, he'd not only answer all her questions but also set her free to sail higher and farther than she could imagine.

But he couldn't.

The temptation of her was too great. Kellan knew himself too well. He'd never be able to keep his hands and mouth off her smooth, pale flesh or keep from plundering her ripe lips. He couldn't deny his tongue and cock the pleasure of her sweet pussy and lush ass.

Fuck, even now he wanted to reach out and take her hand...assure her that he'd lead her down that path of submission she yearned for. Instead, Kellan clutched the steering wheel as he'd done earlier when her vibrant laughter nearly sent him up in flames.

"There isn't a one-size-fits-all answer for you, angel. You have to decide what *you* want from your submission."

"I know what I want…I want to find a *real* Dom who'll teach me the correct ways of the lifestyle, not some made-up bullshit just so he can get his rocks off. Why don't you teach me? I'd work really hard to please and never disappoint you."

Mercy slapped a hand over her mouth, clearly horrified by her request.

Before Kellan could swallow the lump of fear clogging his throat, she lifted the hand from her face and held up her open palm. "Don't answer that. I'm such a… I had no right to put you on the spot like that. Please…forget I said anything. I'm sorry, that was way out of line."

His heart drummed wildly and dread hummed so loudly in his ears he'd barely heard her apology. Feeling as if he'd been punched in the gut, Kellan struggled to fill his lungs—that now seemed weighed in concrete—and nearly missed his turnoff. Hitting the brakes, he whipped the steering wheel to the right and took the exit ramp like a race car driver. By the time he'd coasted to the stoplight, Kellan's heart was still racing, but he'd at least managed to suck in a deep breath.

Mercy was wearing a mortified expression that cut his conscience like a knife.

"I'd love to teach you if I could, angel, but I can't. If you'd like, I'll talk to Mika and see if he can match you up with a Dom who's looking to take on a new sub."

"No. I appreciate your offer, but I don't think I'm ready for a full-time Master."

Thank fuck!

"I didn't mean for such a ridiculous request to fall out of my mouth in the first place," she continued nervously. "It must be the stress of the day or—"

"Mercy," he interrupted. "It wasn't ridiculous. If there was a way I could help teach you, I would. Start attending the sub meetings. You'll find your Master in no time."

It just won't be me.

"I'll try. The dealership was supposed to drop my car off at my apartment today, so I should have wheels to get to the meeting in the morning."

"If not, let me know. Mika and Julianna, er, rather, Emerald live nearby as well. I'm sure they'd be happy to give you a ride."

Pussy! You should take her to the meeting.

He couldn't, and the taunting voice in his head knew why…why he couldn't fill her with false hope…why he had to distance himself from the sassy and hungry submissive.

After Kellan entered Elmhurst Lake's complex, Mercy directed him to her apartment. She even pointed out her blue Camry parked under a covered carport.

"Would you like me to walk you in?"

"No. I'm good." She dismissed his offer with a wave of her hand. "Thank you…for everything Kellan, er, Sir."

He couldn't help but smile as she stumbled over her words. "It was my pleasure. If you see Kerr, shoot first, *then* call the police, understood?"

Her lips curled in a wide smile as she climbed from the car. "I will. Thanks again."

He couldn't help but admire the sexy sway of her hips or the ruby-red shocks of color glistening from the sunlight in her hair as she walked away. Kellan wanted to bolt from the car and follow her into her apartment and show her all the reasons he was the perfect Dominant for her. When Mercy disappeared behind the white door, a wave of guilt sliced him. He mentally began listing off all the reasons he couldn't live out his dreams with her. When Kellan turned out of Mercy's complex, he left behind the fleeting hope of living again.

Glancing at his watch, he mumbled a curse. He was late. Speeding down the street, he turned and ate up the next four blocks quickly. Sadness filled his veins while a boulder of guilt and shame pressed down on his chest. He whipped the sports car beneath the shade of a huge Japanese red maple in the lot of Lake Home Village, cut the engine, and slowly climbed from the car.

At the entrance to the facility, he keyed the code into the touchpad, and waited for the grating buzzer to hum before opening the door. When the receptionist raised her head, Kellan sent her a tight smile as the scent of alcohol and cleaning solvents assaulted his senses.

Forcing his feet down the familiar industrial tiled hall, he paused at the doorway. He bit back the usual howl of anguish clawing the back of his throat as he gazed at the blonde woman sitting in bed, absently staring off into space.

Leena Graham, his wife of twenty-five years, didn't know he'd entered the room…didn't know who he was anymore…didn't know who or where she was, for that matter. Her eyes were fixed on the wall, like always. Kellan would give his dying breath if just once, his vivacious wife—the love of his life—would turn and hit him with that megawatt smile that had knocked him off his feet so long ago.

She didn't…and sadly, she never would.

He struggled to tamp down an onslaught of heartache. Kellan didn't know why now—after five long years—this magnitude of sadness and melancholy had slammed through him. He felt raw and overexposed.

You didn't stop and welcome the rage before you came inside.

No, he hadn't.

Kellan hadn't centered himself with the usual scalding anger and resentment toward the drunk driver who'd stolen Leena's mind and soul when he'd plowed her down in a crosswalk. He took little comfort that the animal responsible for decimating his whole world now sat in a prison cell. In Kellan's eyes, justice had not been served, and never would be. The fact that the cocksucker could still talk and laugh with his loved ones filled Kellan with fury. Life was not fair—a fact he knew well. After all, he lived it daily with piercing bouts of anguish and a catatonic wife who couldn't remember a single day of the love and happiness they'd once shared.

The dazzling light of his Leena's life force had been carelessly extinguished.

Kellan would never see her smile at all the silly things he said.

Never feel her loving arms wrapped around him at the end of the day.

Never taste her soft, passionate kisses.

Never hear her whimper and moan as they poured their love into one another in bed.

Never be able to grow old, side by side.

All he had left were memories and photographs, and endless empty nights.

All Leena had left was an eternity of staring into the blank canvas of oblivion.

Kellan swallowed his misery and inwardly told himself to buck up. He'd wrangle his demons later. Now he needed to savor the precious moments he could spend with his wife.

Striding to the side of Leena's bed, he bent and kissed her cheek. He couldn't help but peer up at her face, holding on to the hope that one day she might respond to his loving gesture…but she didn't. Kellan exhaled as he sat down in the chair beside her bed and gently threaded his fingers through his wife's slender hand. With the pad of his thumb, he caressed her wrist, remembering the heated gaze that lit up her eyes when he'd stroke that sensitive spot.

Fuck!

He was drowning in the same inky dark abyss he'd spent years dragging himself out of. No amount of sorrow or tears would bring Leena back to him—a lesson he'd learned years ago.

"How's my gorgeous girl doing today?" Though Leena never answered, Kellan asked her the same question on each visit, without fail. "Guess what? On the way to work this morning, I heard those songs you bribed me to dance with you to at our senior prom. You remember, don't you? That song by Janet Jackson, 'Miss You Much', and Richard Marx's 'Right Here Waiting'?"

Kellan's throat closed up. He could almost feel her body pressed against his as they slow danced to the latter romantic tune.

He tenderly brushed his knuckles down Leena's cheek.

"I'm still right here waiting for you, love. I always will be." His voice cracked.

Blinking back tears, Kellan sucked in a ragged breath.

"I'm sorry, baby. I'm having a rough one without you today."

Because I think I'm falling in love with someone else. I can't have you both, I know. I have to find a way to walk away from her, but it's so fucking hard. I need you to come back to me, Leena…need you more than you'll ever know.

"My emotions are all over the map."

I'm so fucking lost and lonely without you.

"Don't worry, baby. I'll get my shit together soon."

Or drown in a river of guilt.

"Anyway, back to prom. Remember that god-awful white tux I

rented? Man, I thought I was one suave bastard in that thing. Of course, you couldn't catch me dead in that butt-ugly thing now. But back in the day...you might not have realized it, but you had yourself a stud muffin."

Kellan knew that if she could, Leena would have laughed at his comments.

"And you...whoa, baby. You were looking all fine and shit in that sexy, blue skintight dress, with all those fluffy ruffles on the bottom, and that one sleeve holding it in place. You were looking like every man's wet dream...especially mine. But you were always my dream girl, weren't you?"

Until now. There's another haunting my fantasies and I have no clue how to block her from my brain.

He leaned in close to Leena's ear. "I know I've always been your rock...your Master, but I need you to come back to me, baby...come back and save me, Leena."

"Well, Mr. Kellan. I didn't think we were going to see you today." Lucia, the day nurse who was as tall as she was round, greeted entering the room carrying Leena's afternoon snack tray.

Slamming a lid on his emotions, Kellan stood and took the tray from Lucia with a smile. "I was held up at the courthouse. Since I missed lunch, I wanted to drop by and make sure she gets her snack."

He looked at the items on the tray...applesauce and some kind of pureed meat paste. Though Leena had lost the cognitive skill to chew, she could still swallow. Kellan tried to arrange his docket and free every Friday to spend lunch with his wife, and also give Lucia a small break in her daily routine.

"I'm sure she's happy you're here." Lucia smiled as she tucked a long terry-cloth bib beneath Leena's chin. "Your young lady's had quite a busy day. She had her bath this morning and washed her hair. She wanted to look pretty for your date."

Kellan responded with a small appreciative smile while Lucia softly stroked Leena's hair. After the nurse left the room, he peeled the plastic wrap off the food, picked the spoon from the tray, and sat down beside his wife.

"All right, baby, let's dig in."

Softly cupping Leena's chin, Kellan parted her lips, then eased the spoon onto her tongue. He fed her as he would an infant while her gaze remained fixed to the wall, even lightly scraping up the food that had dribbled onto her lips…the same lips that used to make his blood sing, whether she was kissing him or worshiping his cock.

Stop fucking torturing yourself, asshole, he inwardly berated.

"Paul and Mary send their love," he murmured as he patiently attended his task. "I still remember when the four of us went to Branson. We rented that houseboat and found those kids diving off the cliffs. I thought you were going to dive off the damn boat before Paul even dropped anchor. You were so anxious to climb up that ledge and jump into the lake. Those were good times, weren't they, my love?

"Oh, yeah. Mika sends his love, too. He told me he came by to see you last week. He misses you…" Kellan's voice faded to a whisper. "We all do, girl."

"Daddy? What are you still doing here?" His daughter, Hannah, stood frozen in the doorway. Her face was lined in fear. "Is…is Mom okay?"

His visibly distraught daughter trembled. Kellan quickly set the plate down and wrapped the anxious young woman in his arms.

"She's fine, pumpkin," he assured as he placed a kiss on top of Hannah's head. "I got held up at work and missed our lunch date. So, I came as soon as I could."

Hannah exhaled an audible sigh of relief. Easing from Kellan's arms, she rounded the bed and kissed her mom on the cheek. He watched his twenty-three-year-old daughter brush a tear from her eye as she sat down on the bed beside Leena.

Threading her slender fingers through her mom's golden hair, Hannah smiled. "Hi, Momma. We both came to see you at the same time. I guess we can have a party now. You always loved a good party, right?"

Kellan smiled softly as memories swamped him once more. Unwilling to fall apart in front of his daughter, he pushed them away and resumed feeding Leena. "How are classes going, sunshine?"

"Good," Hannah replied, studying Leena's lax face. "I aced the biology test I'd studied night and day for, which made me happy."

"Excellent."

Hearing his daughter's upbeat voice, Kellan didn't have to force a smile this time.

"I'm…*we're* proud of you, love. Are you still having issues with your lit professor?"

"Ugh," she groaned. "The man's a misogynist. He actually bragged to the class that his failure rate for females was now at ninety percent. I intend to be one of the ten percent who possess a prettier vagina than *his* and pass that stupid class."

Kellan chuckled. "How do you know? Have you *seen* his vagina?"

"Don't make me puke, Dad," she quipped. "Just take my word for it, an elephant's vagina is prettier than his."

"Well, maybe he's not a misogynist at all." Kellan smirked. "Maybe he's suffering from vagina envy."

Hannah tossed her head back and laughed the way Leena used to. "God, I love you, Daddy. I doubt any of the other girls in my sorority talk vaginas with their dads."

"I expect you'll find out before the day is over," Kellan said with a chuckle. "You just keep giving that professor hell, baby."

He didn't need to tell her that. His daughter would give the sexist asshat a run for his money. Hannah was like her parents, not only in looks, with her mother's blonde hair and his striking blue eyes, but she was also headstrong and determined with a zest for life that warmed his heart. His beautiful Hannah was Kellan's pride and joy.

"Oh, I plan to." Her eyes twinkled with mischief the way they used to when she was small.

Kellan was grateful that Hannah had come to visit Leena. His daughter had preempted his morose journey down memory lane, and he'd been able to push Mercy from his mind the rest of his visit. It was only after kissing Leena and Hannah good-bye and leaving the nursing home that the intriguing sub invaded his brain again.

He'd only made it a few blocks before thoughts of Mercy had his cock stirring to life.

He feared the only way to get her out of his system was to fuck her out of it.

Braking for a red light, Kellan cursed and pulled out his cell phone, quickly scrolling through his contacts.

"Fuck! What the hell is her name?" he spat disgustedly. "Natalie! That's it." He punched the number as the light turned green.

One way or another, Kellan was determined to wipe Mercy from his mind.

"Hello," Natalie answered in her usual soft, seductive voice.

"I'm on my way. Be ready in ten minutes."

"Ten minutes? But I just got back from the grocery store and—"

"Either be ready in ten minutes or I'll cancel the lease on the apartment. If groceries are more important to you, maybe it's time we went our separate ways," he growled.

"No. There's no need for that. Are you all right? You sound tense. It's a beautiful day. We could go for a walk or have a picnic in the—"

"This isn't a fucking date. Do I need to recite certain clauses of our contract?"

"No. I-I'll be ready."

"Good. I have thirty minutes. You can deal with your groceries before or after I'm gone. I'll be there shortly."

Kellan hung up the phone as self-loathing squeezed in all around him.

Though Leena had been the love of his life, once he accepted the fact that she was never going to recover, Kellan had to search his soul. His wife might still own his heart, but she could no longer sate his sexual needs. He didn't want to get wrapped up in some messy emotional entanglement. There was too much at risk—like his reputation and livelihood—to pick up random women in bars, so he'd created a profile on a dating site.

Of the women who responded, Natalie seemed mature enough and pragmatic enough to take part in his unorthodox invitation. She also didn't have any qualms about signing the contract and nondisclosure agreement he'd drawn up. In exchange for an apartment and a monthly stipend, Natalie agreed to supply an outlet for Kellan's sexual release.

Right now, he needed that outlet.

As he reached Lake Bluff, shades of calmness began to color his soul, and order and control aligned within before he reached Natalie's apartment.

The late thirty-something brunette with a toned body and dark eyes met him at the door. Kellan stormed in, tugging his tie. After she closed the door behind him, Natalie turned and walked down the hall toward the bedroom. He dropped his gaze to the gentle roll of her hips. Turning off his emotions, Kellan let his primal psyche take over.

By the time he'd reached the bedroom, Natalie lay naked in the center of the mattress, willing and ready. Kellan shucked off his clothes as his cock swelled with blood. He pulled open the bedside table and palmed a condom. Tearing open the foil packet with his teeth, he rolled the latex over himself and crawled onto the bed.

He hovered over her for a long minute. "I'm sorry I was short on the phone…"

"It's okay. Let's make each other feel good."

With a grunt, he drove inside her. Natalie arched and softly moaned. Kellan closed his eyes. He plunged in and out of her snug, hot walls as images of Mercy clutching at his cock filled his mind. A shiver of panic danced up his spine and Kellan quickly opened his eyes. He stared at the pillow beneath Natalie's head and focused on the growing friction engulfing his dick. She wedged a hand between them and strummed her clit until they both orgasmed. A familiar flush lay on her cheeks, and she sent him a soft smile of gratitude.

Natalie's self-esteem had taken a mortal blow when her husband left her for another man some ten plus years ago. Like Kellan, she'd vowed to never love again.

"I'll call you soon," he said over his shoulder as he straightened his tie in the mirror.

"Sounds good," Natalie replied. She rolled out of bed, slid on her robe and tied the sash. "I'll walk you to the door."

Their good-bye was cordial…as usual, just like the recurring emptiness settling deep in his chest as he drove home.

Kellan lessened the void by trying to convince himself that he'd get by with the relief Natalie provided. But he wasn't fooling anyone, not even himself. She was nothing but a stopgap measure…a Band-Aid he kept applying to a gaping, lethal wound that would never heal.

You could have it all with Mercy.

"No," he growled, quickly dismissing the cajoling voice in his head.

He'd already lost his mind around the provocative sub. He couldn't afford to lose his heart to her as well, though in reality, Kellan suspected he already had.

But acting on those feelings was completely out of the question.

CHAPTER THREE

MERCY PATIENTLY STOOD in the foyer of Club Genesis, chatting with her friends Woody and Maple. As the trio waited to be checked in by Dark Desire and his Mistress, Lady Ivory, Mercy kept a tight lid on how she'd passed out in Kellan's arms. There were strict rules about anonymity, so she bit her tongue to protect Sir Justice's true identity. Mercy focused on relaying the disappointing outcome of the trial instead.

"I think Mistress Monique plans to scene with me tonight," Woody announced with glee.

"Really?" Maple smiled. "Are you scared?"

"No. But nervous as hell," he replied quietly. "I don't want to disappoint her."

"Stop. Right. There." Mercy held up her hand. "I didn't want to disappoint Kerr, either, and look what that got me. Be yourself, Woody. If you don't like something she's doing, *tell* her."

"Listen to her, boy," Master Lewis—a Dom who'd been hounding Mercy to scene with him since she'd joined the club—chimed in. "She's right. Open, honest communication is a must in the lifestyle."

"Yes, Sir." Woody nodded.

"Good boy." Lewis turned an expectant smile Mercy's way. "And what about you, sexy Symoné? Are you ready to communicate and negotiate a scene with me yet?"

I'd love to teach you if I could, angel, but I can't. Kellan's words roared in her head, cutting her to the bone with finality she could no longer deny. The Dom she wanted had rebuffed her. He'd done it gently, but he'd refused her all the same. Mercy had to broaden her horizons…start looking at other Doms or her submission could be in jeopardy. She didn't want to be one of the hopeless subs, pining for every Dom who walked by, wearing a *do me* expression.

Lewis didn't hold a candle to Kellan, but sitting around waiting for a miracle, like Justice to cuff her to the cross, was an unattainable fantasy. It was time she started putting her submissive ass into the game.

"Thank you, Sir. I'd be honored to negotiate a scene with you."

Or try. Mercy didn't know the first thing about negotiating a scene.

"Excellent," he all but shouted happily. "I know what that prick Kerr put you through. Trust me. I'll be gentle as a lamb and ease you into subspace slowly. We'll talk more inside the dungeon."

Lewis stepped up to the podium, then with a wink and an even bigger grin, he pushed past the long velvet curtain and was out of sight.

"Did you do that to me on purpose?" Maple whispered tersely.

"Do what?" Mercy asked as Woody presented his driver's license to the couple manning the members list.

"I've been trying to get Lewis to notice me for months," Maple hissed.

"You have?" Mercy blinked in surprise. "Why didn't you tell me?"

"Because I knew you'd steal him from me, like you did Kerr."

A white-hot rage filled Mercy's veins. "Wait a minute. First of all, I would never *steal* a Dom from you or any other sub. Secondly, if I'd known you were interested in Lewis, I would have refused his offer. I've been turning him down nearly every night since we started coming here. And lastly, Kerr used you as much as he did me."

"Forget Kerr," she spat. "You're telling me that Lewis has been sniffing around you this whole time?" Maple huffed as she moved to the podium.

"It's not like I ever encouraged him. I'll fix it."

"*You* don't have to encourage any Dom. They *all* want you! I don't need you doing me any favors. Lewis obviously isn't interested in me. Go on and have fun with him. I'll find another Dom." Maple tossed her nose in the air, turned on her heel, and stormed away.

"Welcome to another drama-filled episode of *As the Dungeon Turns*," Dark Desire, the buff, shirtless sub wearing leather pants and a wide silver collar at his neck, joked in the voice of a game show host.

"Right?" Mercy huffed and handed him her license. Maple's jealous words swirled in Mercy's head. The longer they festered, the more pissed off she became.

"Try to have a good time tonight, Symoné." Lady Ivory flashed a supportive smile.

"Thank you, Ma'am. I will."

When Mercy breached the curtain, Lewis was waiting and practically crawled on top of her. He clutched her elbow and led her deeper into the dungeon. He zinged a barrage of eager questions at her so fast it made her head spin.

Anxiety crawled up her spine while regret pumped in her veins. Why had she agreed to scene with this dude? A slick film oozed from her pores the longer he quizzed her. Mercy's eyes darted over the dungeon, desperately searching for Kellan. She didn't see him anywhere.

"Well? What do you say, girl?" Lewis asked eagerly. "Come on, don't be shy."

"I-I'm sorry, but I don't think I'm really ready to scene after all," she stammered.

"Of course you are. You're just nervous. I give you my word, as a Dom, I will honor your safe word during our scene." Lewis paused only to inhale before continuing. "What is it? Your safe word, I mean. I'll need to know it before we start."

Why?

Did he plan to beat on her until she screamed the word, like Kerr used to do? An icy foreboding filled her. The thought of Lewis' hands caressing her flesh or his cock shoving in and out of her pussy while everyone in the dungeon watched, including Kellan, made her stomach pitch and yaw.

There was only one Dom she wanted to give her submission to, and it certainly wasn't Lewis.

Mercy guided a slightly panicked glance over the dungeon.

Kellan wasn't anywhere.

Jerking from Lewis' grasp, she mumbled an apology, then turned and zigzagged through the members as she raced straight into the ladies' room.

Trembling like a leaf, she paced until she was nearly hyperventilating. Mercy bent over the sink and splashed cold water on her face as she swallowed huge gulps of air. The door suddenly swung open and in rushed Samantha—the former Mistress Sammie who'd traded in her Domme whip for Master Max's submissive collar. She moved in behind

Mercy and gently rubbed her back.

"What's wrong, Symoné? I saw you tear ass in here, pale and shaking like you'd seen a ghost. Kerr hasn't somehow snuck inside the club, has he?"

"No." Mercy grabbed a handful of paper towels and wiped her face.

"Good. I was in Mika's office earlier when Sir Justice came in and filled him in on what happened at the courthouse today. It just burns my ass that stupid judge didn't lock that animal away."

"Kellan's here?"

"Kellan, huh?" Samantha smirked. "Yes, but I haven't seen *Sir Justice* come down from Mika's office yet. He's probably still up there. Tell me what happened in the dungeon that upset you?"

"Nothing. Something. I don't know. I probably freaked out for nothing."

"Come with me." Samantha gently urged her toward the door.

Mercy dug in her heels and shook her head. "I don't want to go out there yet."

"I wasn't taking you back to the dungeon but to my room for some girl talk."

"Oh, that would be nice."

Mercy followed Samantha out the restroom and down the long hall of private rooms. As they reached their destination, a warm body eased in alongside Mercy. She tensed, fearing Lewis didn't want to give up his quest and had followed her to press her to play again. When she looked over her shoulder, it wasn't Lewis peering down at her but Kellan. His expression told her he was pissed and ready to spit nails.

Before she could even greet the man, he clutched her elbow and scowled. "What did Lewis say that upset you?"

His touch ignited that heated sexual awakening inside her again. The man was like a walking, talking aphrodisiac.

"Nothing."

"Do *not* lie to me, angel. What did he say?"

"He wanted to scene with me, like always. Lewis has been pestering me since I joined the club. When he asked me again tonight in the foyer, I told him I would—"

"So you're going to let Lewis scene with you?"

Kellan's tone was dripping with sarcasm…or was it jealousy? Why did he even care? It wasn't like Sir Justice would cuff her to a cross and play with her.

"I was, but I decided not to."

Samantha didn't say a word. She simply darted glances between them before unlocking the door.

"Thank you, Samantha. I'll take it from here." Kellan all but dismissed the other sub as he kicked out a foot, keeping the door propped open.

"Stay as long as you'd like, Sir." A knowing smile tugged the corners of Samantha's lips. "I'll be at the bar if either of you need me."

"Wait. I thought you and I were going to talk." Mercy hated the tone of panic in her voice.

"This won't take long," Kellan drawled.

Samantha nodded. She gave Mercy a supportive wink and walked away.

Kellan led her inside the room and sat down on the bed, dragging Mercy down beside him.

"I take it Lewis berated you for changing your mind."

"No."

"All right. What exactly *did* he say that frightened you?"

"He wanted to know my safe word."

"And?" Justice pressed, wearing a look of confusion.

"And it scared me. I mean, the only reason he'd need to know that was if he intended to whale me until I had to use it. I may be naïve when it comes to certain aspects of the lifestyle, but I'm not stupid. No way am I going to let some Dom I hardly know strap me to a cross and do as he pleases."

Kellan issued a soft chuckle.

"What's so funny?" Mercy bristled.

"Nothing. I just adore your spunk." He quickly sobered. "You shouldn't let *any* Dom do as he pleases. That's what negotiations are for. As for your safe word, never scene with a Dom who doesn't know what it is. It's the only way they'll know if you're in trouble and need to pause or stop the scene altogether."

"I didn't think of it like that." She dropped her head and let out a long groan.

"What did you think a safe word was for?"

"Kerr told me to use it when I couldn't take any more pain."

"I take it you never negotiated your scenes with him."

She shook her head. "No. He'd just order me to bend over and to shut up until he was done. I don't even know *how* to negotiate a scene."

Kellan closed his eyes and inhaled deeply. His nostrils flared and his lips thinned into a tight line. After several long seconds, he mumbled a curse, then locked on to her with an uncompromising stare.

"I'll pick you up at seven thirty in the morning so you can attend the sub meeting. We'll grab breakfast, then come to the club. Understood?"

Mercy nodded. The adamant tone in his instructions slid over her flesh like warm honey. This was the kind of control she ached for him to give her. Her nipples drew up tight and hard, throbbing in time with the growing ache between her legs. The overwhelming need for his Dominance was burning her alive, but it was more than that. She craved this man with a primitive, visceral hunger. Mercy feared that if she couldn't convince him to put out the submissive wildfire inside her, she'd soon turn to nothing but ash.

What was stopping him? Why wouldn't he take her out to the dungeon and start teaching her how to please him? Was she not attractive enough? Did he want an experienced sub? Was their age difference too much for him to handle?

All Kellan had told her was that he couldn't train her. But he hadn't gone into any detail…hadn't given her a tangible reason for his refusal. The not knowing *why* ate at her soul.

Mercy had had enough…enough second-guessing her desirability as a sub and as a woman…enough of filling her head with a plethora of questions. She wanted answers, dammit. And she aimed to get them.

Gathering her courage, she lifted her chin and stared him in the eyes. "Tell me why you can't you train me. If it's because you have socks older than me, let me assure you, I'm emotionally mature enough to handle your Dominance."

His expression softened. "It's not about age."

"Then what is it? If I'm not submissive enough, I'll work harder. I'll learn anything you want to teach me. If you don't like my hair, my makeup, my clothes…I'll change. Just *please*…give me a chance to show you what's in my heart."

Pride be damned, Mercy didn't care that she was begging. The submissive within ached to beg longer and harder…to stir his Dominance enough that he would take control and light her dark, confusing path.

Kellan tensed. A savage noise, like a strangled roar, rumbled deep in his chest. His expression hardened, twisting with a look of pain, while fire and hunger blazed in his eyes. He urgently cupped her nape and dragged her to his mouth, claiming her in a passionate kiss.

Electricity shot through her, setting fire to every cell in her body.

His lips were warm, firm, and ravenous as he devoured her.

Mercy fell limp in his arms.

She whimpered and kissed him back, striving to return the blissful, palpable hunger he bathed her in.

Her pulse thundered in her ears.

Kellan dragged his tongue over the seam of her lips.

Mercy moaned and opened, welcoming him inside.

His kiss grew raw…urgent.

Their tongues tangled in slick, wet warmth.

His masculine scent made her dizzy.

Mercy's body pulsed and throbbed beneath tingling skin.

She was lost…lost in the texture and taste of this magnificent man.

Kellan wrapped one broad hand beneath her breast.

Through the corset, the heat of his touch singed her skin.

Her clit throbbed.

Her nipples ached and strained.

She clutched his shoulders. Absorbing the heat rolling off him, she held on for dear life.

Arching into his palm, she ached to feel him glide his thumb over her swollen peaks.

She needed something more…needed Kellan to strum the need away…or rev it higher. At the moment, Mercy didn't know which…didn't care.

But Kellan did. He knew exactly what she needed.

He brushed her pebbled tip and swallowed her moan of delight.

Answering her call, he groaned and cupped her breast.

Without warning, he tore from her mouth and jerked his hand back as if she'd burned him with acid.

His eyes widened. Like a kaleidoscope, a million emotions swirled over his face. But it was the blatant look of horror that landed the crushing blow to the bonfire blazing inside her.

Mercy found it even more disenchanting when Kellan vaulted off the bed and rushed to the door.

"I'll pick you up in the morning."

Mercy blinked, and he was gone.

She drew her fingers to her mouth.

The door shut with a brutal finality.

The tingle of his kiss still lingered on her lips.

Shock, disappointment, and confusion pinged through her.

Rage trumped them all and soared like a rocket inside her.

"What. The. Fuck?" she railed. "He kisses me till my damn toes curl, sets me on fire, and then runs out the goddamn door? Seriously? What kind of game is this asshat playing?"

Bolting off the bed, Mercy paced. Desperate to make sense of Kellan's kiss and abrupt exodus, she couldn't. She was too focused on the hot, pulsating throb enveloping her body.

"Argh!" she growled. "What the hell am I doing here?"

Mercy flopped down on the bed and covered her face with her hands.

The night had turned into a complete clusterfuck.

She'd come to the club to spend time with the other subs, watch and learn from the various sessions, and hopefully get a hello from Kellan. While she'd enjoyed his kiss far more than a simple hello, him running out of the room like his ass was on fire completely baffled her.

She looked at the door and heaved a disgruntled sigh. Though the idea of staying in Samantha's room all night held a world of appeal, Mercy owed Lewis an apology. A shiver slithered through her. Having to be near the man again made her skin crawl. She'd rather spend the evening next to Kellan.

Touching a finger to her lips once more, Mercy closed her eyes and replayed his potent kiss in her mind.

"Dammit! Why did he leave?" she groused out loud. "We could have been sweating and writhing by now. I could have my legs wrapped around him while he fed his fat cock inside me…stretching me…filling me, until we both exploded in screaming ecstasy."

Mercy slammed her fist onto the mattress and stood. Pacing, she tried to work off her mix of anger and lust.

"Oh, fuck this!"

With a snarl, she opened the door and marched down the hall only to be met by several couples heading to their private rooms for BDSM fun. A pang of envy sliced her heart. When she stepped into the dungeon, the sights and sounds of subs finding their contentment only increased her surly mood.

She quickly convinced herself that the night was a lost cause and decided to just go home. A hot bubble bath and a couple glasses of wine sounded far more appealing than waiting, wishing, and praying that Kellan would sweep her off her feet and bind her to a cross or spanking bench.

Dammit!

She was beyond pathetic.

Mercy was well on her way to a full-blown pity party complete with cake, streamers, and helium-filled balloons. The only things missing were the jugglers and clowns.

With her head down, avoiding the members' eyes, she pushed past the velvet curtain only to run straight into Savannah and her two Masters, Nick and Dylan.

Though Savannah had become a trusted friend—after she and her Masters along with Samantha's Master, Max had rescued Mercy from Kerr's club—the fact that Savannah had *two* Masters when Mercy couldn't manage to entice a single one chafed.

"You're not leaving already, are you, Symoné?" Savannah frowned.

"Yeah. I'm just…not feeling it tonight."

"May I have a few minutes to talk to Symoné, please?" Savannah shot her Masters a pleading glance.

The two rugged Doms nodded in tandem.

"We'll meet you inside, kitten," Dylan stated before he and Nick disappeared into the dungeon.

Mercy followed Savannah to a quiet corner in the far lobby away from the members waiting to be checked in. At a small table surrounded by leather padded chairs, the two women sat down.

A look of concern was stamped over Savannah's face. "What's going on?"

"Like I said, I'm just not feeling it." Mercy shrugged.

"I'm not buying it. Spill, sister."

"Fine." Mercy knew she was a terrible liar. "Lewis was all up in my shit again, only this time, I caved."

"You scened with him?" Savannah's eyes widened.

"No. I changed my mind."

Over the next several minutes, Mercy filled her friend in on all the gory details of the evening, ending with Justice's earth-shattering kiss and beeline out the door. When she was done, Savannah sat back wearing a shit-eating grin.

"Sir Justice likes you. But it sounds like he's not sure what to do about it."

"That's just it. He's not going to do *anything* about it…ever!"

"Give him some time to figure it out. I have a feeling he'll come around."

Mercy shook her head. "No. I've done everything but strip off my clothes and do a damn pole dance. He's *not* interested."

Then what was that sizzling kiss about?

Mercy didn't have a clue. She was too obsessed with the depressing aftermath.

"Look, I've kept you from your Masters long enough. Enjoy your night. I'm going home."

Even before Savannah's eyes drifted over Mercy's shoulders, she knew Kellan was near. As usual, the hairs on the back of her neck stood on end, and a thrill shot up her spine. It was as if he'd hard-wired her body with a silent alarm system rigged to go off every time he drilled her with his dissecting stare. She found the sensation unnerving yet oddly comforting in ways she couldn't unravel.

"Don't look now," Savannah whispered. "But Mister Kiss and Run is standing by the podium behind you, watching you like a hawk. Come back inside the dungeon. You can sit with Masters and me."

Mercy gave a barely perceptible shake of her head. "Thanks, but it's been a crazy, confusing, and ungodly stressful day. I should have just stayed home and snuggled up on the couch in my jammies."

"Oh, my god, that's right. Today was the trial. What happened with Kerr?"

"I lost. He's free to trap and terrorize subs to his heart's content."

"I'm sorry. Dammit. That truly sucks. If you need to talk or just hang out or anything…call me, okay? I'll even help you try to sort things out with…" Savannah subtly lifted her chin toward Kellan.

"There's nothing to sort out there…but I'll call. Maybe we can grab lunch again soon."

"Yes. Let's do it." Savannah nodded excitedly as she stood. After bending to give Mercy a hug, she hurried away.

Trying to steady her nerves, Mercy stayed in her seat, staring at a blank wall for several long minutes. Kellan's stare warmed her from the inside out. The clawing ache to feel his lips and hands on her again made her want to scream. Instead, she stood and darted a glance over her shoulder. Kellan was leaning against the wall, arms crossed over his sturdy chest, and blue eyes searing her with a hungry stare. She zeroed in on his lips and her pulse tripled. Mercy wanted to climb his long, sinewy body, like King Kong did the Empire State Building, wrap her arms and legs around Kellan, and kiss him until all the chaos inside her calmed. Though the idea was tempting as hell, it wouldn't cure her hopeless infatuation only convince him she was pathetic. No, attacking the man wouldn't change her hopeless situation.

Forcing a weak smile, Mercy sent him a slight nod, then set her sights on the front door. As she weaved her way through the members, Kellan's stare raked her back, sending goose bumps to explode over her arms.

When she stepped from the club, the cold night air pierced her flesh like needles. Mercy tucked her head and ran toward her car, digging the key from her pocket. From out of nowhere, she felt a hand grip her arm. Before she could process what was happening, she was being roughly spun around and found herself face-to-face with Kerr.

Like a bomb, fear exploded inside her.

"Get your hands off me!"

Her indignant tone only made his lecherous smile widen.

"I don't think so, sweetheart," Kerr growled.

He tightened his grip and yanked her toward him. Mercy felt something hard poking at her ribs. She looked down and saw the barrel of a gun pressed at her side.

"My hands on you are the least of your worries. We have some business to settle, you and me."

Panic swelled like a tsunami. Mercy darted a terrified glance at the camera mounted over the door of the club. At that exact moment, Kellan stepped outside. When he saw Kerr gripping her arm, fury engulfed his face.

Mercy prayed Kellan could see the gun and wouldn't try anything heroically stupid. Whatever Kerr had planned for her, she wanted to believe she could survive. But helplessly watching him kill the man she loved would rip her to shreds.

Loved?

Even in the face of such dire circumstances, Mercy almost laughed. It had taken an ugly act of violence for her to realize she'd fucked up and fallen in love with a man who didn't want her.

It was Murphy's Law at its finest.

"Symoné, I need you to come back inside with me. Now!" Kellan barked.

"She's not going to be able to accommodate your *order* this time, Judge," Kerr stated flatly. He lifted the gun to Mercy's head and grinned. "If you don't turn around and walk away, I'll splatter her brains all over the sidewalk. That's the truth, the whole truth, and nothing but the truth, so help me God."

Numbed from the cold and fear, her body shook. A whimper leaked from her lips as she silently pleaded for Kellan to follow Kerr's instructions. But before Kellan could move a muscle, the door to the club burst open. Mika and two muscle-bound DMs raced onto the sidewalk.

"Drop the gun, Kerr. You can't kill her now; you've got too many witnesses." Kellan's voice was as hard as steel and as arctic as ice. "Let her go!"

In the distance, Mercy could hear sirens screaming. Tears slid down her cheeks. She was terrified the madman would kill her before help arrived.

Kerr tensed. Only he wasn't the Kerr she'd once known. This man was a monster. A fact confirmed by the wild look in his eyes. Frozen in fear, she watched as more members poured from the club. Their gasps and murmurs filled her with even more fear.

"You heard the man," Mika bellowed as he raised a gun of his own and quickly chambered a bullet. "Let her go, or I'll blow your head off, Kerr. Hear those sirens? The cops are coming for you. Put the gun down, or be hauled off in a body bag. It's up to you."

Fear flashed in Kerr's eyes. His face contorted in hate and fury.

"You're not worth going to jail for, cunt," he spat in a low demonic voice. "But don't worry, Symoné…I'll be back to drain the life out of you soon."

With a mighty shove, Kerr sent her sprawling to the pavement. The concrete chewed her shoulder and arm. Pain exploded inside her skull and lights flashed behind her eyes when her head bounced off the cement.

A cacophony of footsteps—running away and racing toward her—pelted Mercy's brain like sledgehammers.

Kellan gathered her into his arms and cradled her to his chest.

"I've got you, angel. I've got you," he whispered in a voice rife with anguish.

Swaddled in the safety of his arms, she curled in, soaking up the heat of his body. She pressed her head against him as his whispered words rumbled deep in his chest.

"Get her inside, Kell." Mika's voice shook with rage. Mercy blinked up at the club owner as he stood and turned, then bellowed, "Somebody find Brooks and get him out here, stat!"

She knew Mika was only trying to help, but his yell crashed through her skull like a gong. Mercy closed her eyes and cringed.

"You're not going to pass out on me again, are you?" Kellan whispered.

Obviously he was trying to lighten the mood, but the worry in his eyes and the grimace stretched over his lips didn't hold an ounce of humor.

"No, Sir. I'm going to stay awake in hopes that you'll kiss me again."

Kellan stood and lifted her off the ground. Mercy pressed a palm to her forehead and squeezed her eyes shut.

"I should spank your ass red for leaving the club alone. You scared twenty years off my life…twenty years I don't have to spare," he quietly scolded as he carried her inside.

"Please…spank away," she murmured for his ears only.

"You're an incorrigible little minx."

While her sassy plea lessened the fear marring his face, it didn't completely erase his angst.

"Where do you hurt, Symoné?" physician and Master Sam Brooks—who'd patched her up after her first altercation with Kerr—asked as he moved in alongside Kellan.

"Everywhere," Mercy groaned. "My head feels like it's going to explode, and my elbow's on fire. My hip and shoulder, too."

"Okay. Let me take a quick look at you. Justice, would you lay her down here on the carpet for a minute? We can move her to my private room if we need to."

"We've got to stop meeting like this, Master Sam," Mercy hissed as Kellan eased her to the floor. "Your girl's going to think I'm trying to hit on you."

"I know better," his submissive, Cindy, assured with a soft smile. She crouched next to her Master before placing several items on the ground out of Mercy's sight. "Someone needs to put a hit out on Kerr and end our misery."

"Mika was ready to do that if Kerr would have pulled the trigger."

"But then we would have lost you." Cindy frowned. "That's not a trade any of us would ever make."

"No. No. No." Savannah pushed through the crowd sobbing.

"I'm okay," Mercy assured, watching tears roll down her friend's face. "There's no blood this time. I'm good."

"I'm afraid there is, angel," Kellan corrected.

She glanced at Brooks, watching silently as he and Cindy pulled on white surgical gloves. It was then that Mercy realized Kellan was still supporting her neck. Streaks of blood were smeared over his white cotton shirt.

"Is the blood coming from my shoulder or my elbow?" Mercy asked.

"I'm going to sit you up. Let me know right away if you're going to be sick," Brooks instructed, ignoring her question.

"Okay." Mercy pinned Kellan with an anxious stare. "Where am I bleeding?"

"From the back of your head, angel. Don't worry. Sam will get you fixed up. He's the best surgeon we've got."

"I'm the only surgeon you've got here," Brooks chuckled.

"That's why you're the best," Mercy chimed in.

"Damn right it is." Brooks flashed her a wide grin before turning somber and focusing his attention on the back of her head.

She could feel him carefully smoothing back sections of her hair.

"No stiches, Doc. I'm not letting anyone shave my head," Mercy protested.

"If you need them, Sam will be shaving your head without any argument," Kellan scolded.

His unyielding tone filled her with a warm glow. If only he would take the initiative, Mercy was ready and willing to heed his every command.

"Kerr did this to her?" Mellie, Savannah's older sister, asked in a tone filled with shock.

"Yes. He's gone and lost his fuc...his damn mind," Samantha bit out angrily. "Was he like this when you were his sub?"

Mercy turned her head to see who the hell Sanna was talking to. When Mellie bit her lip and shook her head, Mercy blinked in utter shock.

"You...you were with Kerr?"

"Years ago," Mellie explained. "When I lived in Kansas City. He was always an ass, but he wasn't violent. What happened to him?"

So it isn't just me who's noticed a change in him. Maybe he really is crazy now.

While neither woman could explain his bizarre behavior, Mercy found comfort in the fact that his menacing actions weren't all in her mind.

Sam pressed something cold and stingy against her scalp. "This might burn a little."

"Ouch." She dug her fingernails into Kellan's arm. "A little? Try a lot."

"Necessary evil," Sam mumbled. "I need to clean this up so I can take a better look."

"Easy with the claws, kitten, or you'll soon have us both bleeding," Kellan warned with a crooked grin.

Mercy jerked her fingers away. "Sorry."

"I'm only kidding, angel." He clasped his hand around her wrist and placed her fingers back on his arm. "I can take it."

"That's my line...when you spank me, Sir."

Her taunting remark wasn't meant to entice him, not really. She was trying to tame the residual fear thrumming inside her. It wasn't every day a madman pressed a gun to her head or made her realize that she'd fallen in love...like an idiot.

A look of animalistic lust flared over Kellan's face, erasing the lines of worry previously etched there. "Damn it, angel," he muttered under his breath.

Without warning, her stomach lurched and her mouth began to water. "Back up. Back up!"

"What's wrong?" he asked.

"I'm going to be sick."

Kellan grabbed a towel from the floor, gathered the corners in a lose fist, and held the fabric under her chin. Mercy shot him a wide-eyed *you've got to be shitting me* expression as the contents of her dinner began roiling upward.

"Here." Savannah's Master, Nick shoved a trashcan between Mercy's legs.

She clutched the lined bucket and proceeded to toss her cookies.

"Sam?" Kellan's voice was rife with uneasiness.

"Time to take her to the ER just to be safe," the doctor replied.

"I don't want to go to the hospital," Mercy moaned.

"Too bad. You're going and I'm driving you there."

Kellan's uncompromising tone would have made her shiver if she weren't blowing chow in a trashcan and her head wasn't throbbing like a bitch.

Mercy lifted her eyes and glanced around the people hovering around her as Brooks wrapped her head in gauze. Master Lewis had Maple—who was wearing a look of sorrow—clutched at his side.

A tiny, satisfied smile crept over Mercy's lips.

"I'm sorry," Maple mouthed. Tears welled in her eyes.

"It's okay," Mercy whispered.

"Yes, girl. You're going to be just fine," Brooks assured, unaware she'd been talking to Maple. "Once we reach the ER, we'll get you something for the pain. Can you stand up?"

Mercy nodded, then groaned as a new wave of pain reverberated in her brain.

Before she'd even attempted to move, Kellan lifted her off the floor and back into his arms. Mercy rested her head on his chest, needing the reassurance and comfort he offered. When they reached the foyer, Mika was talking with three uniformed officers. Kellan tensed when the cops looked his way and did a double take. Clearly, they were surprised to see the Honorable Judge Kellan Graham inside a kink club.

"I'm taking Miss O'Connor to Highland Park Hospital," Kellan stated flatly. "She can answer your questions there, when she's able."

"We'll be there shortly, Judge." An older officer nodded curtly.

Kellan's anonymity had been shattered because of her.

A wave of guilt crashed through Mercy as he carried her out the door. He eased her into the passenger seat of his car before sprinting around the vehicle and sliding in behind the wheel.

"Oh, god. I'm so sorry."

"Don't worry about it, angel," Kellan said.

"How can I not? It's my fault you were recognized at the club."

"No. It's not your fault. I could have sought refuge in one of the members' rooms while Mika or Sam drove you to the hospital. I outed myself. It was my own choice."

"What happens now?"

Kellan shrugged. "Nothing. I'll talk to Officer Amblin at the hospital. He'll take care of everything. Don't worry. All I want you focusing on is getting better."

"As soon as this headache goes away, I'll be fine."

Kellan reached down and threaded his fingers through hers as he sped toward the hospital. Mercy wondered if she'd ever grow accustomed to the inexplicable heat that raced through her when he touched her. She hoped not.

When he turned onto one of the busier thoroughfares, the headlights of oncoming traffic pierced her skull like a knife. Mercy closed her eyes and drifted off to sleep.

"Come on, angel. You have to wake up." Kellan's insistent tone pulled her from the darkness and resonated in her ears like a damn foghorn.

"Stop yelling," she groaned. "I'm awake."

"Then open your eyes."

"I can't. The light hurts."

"Okay, but you're going to have to talk to me so you don't try to go back to sleep."

"God, you're bossy," she groused.

"Thank you. It's my job."

Mercy felt his smile in the tone of his words.

"You pick the topic. My head hurts too bad to think."

"Tell me about growing up in Texas. Did you have horses?"

"Uh-huh. A pretty tan-and-white mare named Abigail. She was surefooted and fast as the wind."

"Do you still ride?"

"Around here? Not hardly," Mercy snorted. She immediately regretted the action and cupped her forehead. "I wish. I miss it."

"There's a place in Peoria where I like to ride. It's called Coyote Trails. I'll take you there once you've healed."

"Really?" Her eyes flew open wide. She regretted that move as well and quickly snapped her lids shut. "That would be wonderful. How long have you been riding?"

"Years. I love it."

"Where did you grow up, Kellan?"

"Sun Valley. It's a small town in Idaho on the southwest edge of the Salmon-Challis National Forest. I spent a lot of time snow skiing in the winter and fishing in the summer."

"I love to fish. God, I haven't fished in forever," she said on a wistful sigh. "When I go home for Christmas, I'm going to do both...ride and fish."

"That sounds like a wonderful vacation."

"You should come with me for Christmas," she blurted out unexpectedly, followed by an inward groan.

The man doesn't want to teach you submission or probably even kiss you again. He sure as hell isn't going to spend Christmas with you and your wild family.

"What?" Kellan choked.

"Nothing. It's the pain talking. Just ignore me."

"I wish I could, angel, but I can't," he mumbled under his breath.

"Can't what? Come for Christmas or ignore me?"

"Both."

His confession ignited a flicker of hope inside her. Self-preservation warned to keep the flame no more than a sputter, or she'd be dealing with more than a bitchin' headache.

When Kellan pulled up to the entrance of the ER, he squeezed her hand. "Sit tight. I'll get a wheelchair."

"I can walk."

"I know you *can*, but you're not going to. Understand?"

"Yes, Sir." Though she grumbled her reply, Mercy savored the Dominant command he unknowingly sprinkled over her.

CHAPTER FOUR

KELLAN STARED AT the beautiful sub as she lay, eyes closed, in the dimly lit exam room. She looked so fragile, so vulnerable, but Mercy was a trooper. After answering officer Amblin's questions and filing yet another assault charge against Kerr, she was sent off for a cat scan. He'd been climbing the walls for hours, though he'd somehow maintained a calm outward veneer. He couldn't shut off his brain…couldn't keep from projecting gruesome forms of torture Kerr might have inflicted had Kellan not followed her out of the club.

A crushing helplessness settled deep in his bones.

He didn't know how to keep her at arm's length and safe at the same time.

It didn't help that for the second time today, he was perched next to a hospital bed—first next to Leena, and now beside Mercy—being chewed alive beneath the jaws of powerlessness. Being chained and bound to circumstances beyond his control left him feeling weak and impotent.

He was a fucking Dom! But the goddamn stars kept aligning themselves in ways that tested his command at every turn. Kellan knew it wasn't only his command that was being tested but his resolve as well.

Mercy dented his Dominant armor in ways no other submissive ever had. He had no business harboring such intense feelings for the girl, but again…he was powerless to block her from his brain and his heart.

Of course, if Leena were still with him, mentally, this bloody battle inside him wouldn't be raging. Kellan wouldn't have even looked twice at Mercy.

Guilt stabbed deep.

Everything he wanted to do to the girl was wrong on every moral level.

Kellan bit back a howl of frustration and dragged a hand through his hair.

He shouldn't be here.

Shouldn't be tempting himself with what he couldn't have, and he sure as fuck shouldn't have kissed her. He scoffed inwardly. It was the single stupidest thing he'd done in years. He foolishly convinced himself that if he simply sated his curiosity and tasted those plump, sweet lips of hers, he could purge her from his system.

Idiot.

All he'd accomplished was fanning the embers of desire into a roaring inferno he'd never be able to put out.

Her lips were as soft as velvet, her tongue like silk. He could live to be a million and still not wipe the taste of her from his soul. She was branded in his psyche now, and nothing he could do or say would change that.

Could he live with only the memory of that one incredible moment when he'd claimed her mouth without going insane?

Good luck.

Even his subconscious knew it wasn't possible.

It had been five grueling years since he'd kissed a woman with such mind-blowing passion. Mercy had made him feel alive once more. Kellan wanted to savor that awakening. Strip her naked and drown in her lush body more than he'd wanted his next breath. Remembering the feel of her hard, pointed nipple on his thumb was a hell all its own. But dammit, he couldn't lead her on and he certainly couldn't continue to keep mind-fucking himself. Somehow, he had to find the strength to fight his overwhelming attraction to Mercy.

It wasn't fair to her, him, or Leena.

He'd made a vow, twenty-five years ago, to love, honor, and respect…until death parted them. The empty years without Leena had made him weak. He'd bent his vow as far as he could. While Kellan wasn't proud that he'd drawn up a purely physical contract with Natalie, slaking his sexual needs with her was worlds apart from the way his soul slipped away when he sank inside Mercy's mouth. He couldn't allow the still roaring blaze inside to consume him.

The realization of how brutally he'd tarnished his promise to Leena terrified Kellan.

He'd all but welcomed Mercy to bring chaos and craving to his rational and orderly world. He had to put the brakes on now, or heaven help him, she'd wreck him all the way to his soul.

"Good news," Brooks announced as he strolled into the exam room. "There's no sign of any brain bleeds or broken bones. That bump on the back of your head will be sore, but no stitches were necessary. I know you're happy about that. You do have a slight concussion, which explains your wicked headache."

"I don't have a headache…not anymore," Mercy slurred. Her eyes were barely slit open. "Whatever you gave me is workin' juss' fine."

Kellan wanted to laugh at the drugged-out crooked smile curled on her mouth.

"I'm afraid when that shot wears off, you'll be singing a different tune." Brooks grinned as he handed Kellan a stack of papers and a small bag. "I raided the drug cabinet. You've got plenty of pain meds to get her through the night. There's a prescription for more in the bag if she should needs them. For tonight, though, you'll need to wake her every four hours. If she's in pain, you can give her one or two pills, but no more than two every four hours. Other than that, you're free to take her home."

You'll need to wake her every four hours. You'll need to wake her every four hours.

Brooks' instructions spooled through Kellan's head as a wave of panic spilled through him. His sole focus had been on getting Mercy the medical attention she needed. He hadn't even thought about what he would do with her after they left the hospital…until now.

You didn't suppose you could just drop her off at her apartment and drive away, did you? the little voice in the back of his head mocked.

No. He hadn't supposed *anything!* That was the problem.

The fact that he'd be spending the night, sleeping under the same fucking roof as Mercy, gave new meaning to the word *control*.

He was so fucked.

While his heart tried to leap out of his chest, Kellan nodded to Brooks.

"I'll take her home with me and keep a close eye on her." Though the words rolled off his tongue easily enough, Kellan's gut twisted.

He'd just made the most potentially dangerous decision of his life. Even Mercy turned a glassy-eyed stare at him that screamed, *Are you fucking crazy?*

Probably. But *she* was the cause of his insanity.

"You don't have to babysit me, Kellan. I can set an alarm and take my meds like a big girl."

"I'm sure you can," Brooks replied in a placating tone he probably reserved for children and patients high on pain meds. "But you have no business being alone tonight. You need to be fully awakened every four hours." The doctor then turned a serious expression toward Kellan. "Make sure she wakes up. If you can't—"

"If I can't wake her, I'll call 911. I know the drill. Believe me, I'm not taking any chances with her safety. I had a couple concussions playing football back in high school."

"All right." Brooks pinned Mercy with a stern and serious glare. "Now for the part you won't like. No driving, reading, television, computers, or other electronics for at least a week. You need to let your brain and body rest."

"A week?" Mercy gasped.

"A week…at least," Brooks repeated.

"Yes, Sir." She scowled.

Kellan studied her carefully. It might have been the drugs, but Mercy had given in way too easily. If she thought she was going to blow off Sam's orders, Kellan had news for his feisty live-in—*good god, what have I done?*—patient.

He intended to keep Mercy's sassy ass on the straight and narrow even if he had to tie her to the bed.

The idea made his cock stir to life; but then she always managed to make him hard enough to pound railroad spikes by just breathing.

Son of a bitch!

The drive to Kellan's home was…enlightening.

Mercy was so whacked out on pain meds she rambled non-stop. Her lack of filter was educational and amusing as hell. There were times it was all he could do not to laugh out loud, but that might have caused her to be quiet. That's the last thing Kellan wanted.

"I mean, pepperoni pizza is the bomb, but nothing beats a calzone…if it's made right, that is. Some places don't know how to cook 'em. The insides are all doughy and gross. It tastes nasty that way, you know?"

"Uh-huh." He smirked.

"What's your favorite food?"

"Steak."

"Oh, I love steak. Mmm!"

The low, sultry moan that bubbled from the back of her throat made Kellan want to pull over, unzip his pants, and make her fucking scream.

"I love all kinds of meat, actually," she continued.

I have some hot, hard meat you can wrap your pretty lips around, right here, angel.

Kellan frowned at the pubescent thoughts swirling in his head. Even if he *could* bring to life the images filling his mind, like a kick-ass porn flick, Mercy wasn't in any shape to play the starring role the way he wanted.

A hot shower and his fist were the only relief to be found for the boner Kellan was sporting…after he had Mercy settled in his guest room and fast asleep.

"How long have you been in the lifestyle?" Before he could answer, Mercy continued. "I bet forever. You've got that Dom vibe down pat. It's"—she sighed wistfully—"intimidating in a deliciously naughty sort of way. But you know that I mean, you know you ooze command, right? I still don't get it, Kellan. Why won't you train me? Do you already have a sub you're hiding?"

Oh, fuck. Not this again.

Kellan didn't know what to say. He wasn't going to lie, but this wasn't the time or the place to start discussing Leena. Hopefully, if he was lucky, Mercy wouldn't remember any of this conversation in the morning.

"You've already asked me why I won't train you."

"I know," she replied as if he were thick as a stump. "But you won't answer me. Will you answer me now?"

"No."

"That's it? That's all you're going to say?"

"Yes."

"You're nothing but a big ol' party pooper, judge, jury, and justice, Sir."

Kellan bit his tongue to keep from laughing. When she stuck out her bottom lip in an exaggerated pout, he clamped down even harder to keep from groaning. Christ, he wanted to suck that luscious plump flesh between his teeth and feast on her mouth for days.

Focus! You're driving.

"So how many subs have you had?"

"One."

"Just one?" Mercy blinked in surprise. "What happened? No, never mind. You won't tell me anyway. I should just shut up and stop asking questions." Mercy paused long enough to draw in another breath before she was off again. "Did she leave you? Or did you release her? Does she live here in Chicago? How long have you lived in Chicago, by the way?"

Kellan cracked a smile. She reminded him of Hannah when she was three. His daughter was a magpie who asked more questions than there were minutes in a year.

"Aw, come on. Don't be a poop. You know all kinds of things about me," Mercy drawled.

She twisted in her seat and leaned forward, flashing him a mischievous grin.

God, she was so damn adorable.

"You're quite a puzzle, Kellan Graham, but I'm determined to figure you out...one of these days."

"You are, huh?"

"Oh, yeah. I wanna know what flips your buttons, floats your boat, and makes you tick."

You!

"Why do people say that all the time? I mean, nobody really ticks," she pondered aloud. "And why wouldn't a boat float...unless it had a hole in it? But then it would just sink. Right?"

"It would."

Mercy paused. He could feel her staring at him but kept his eyes on the road.

"Why are you being so nice to me? I mean...you usually act like I piss you off. You're always snarly and grouchy...well, except for when Kerr's around. Then you're like a knight on a white horse."

"I'm no knight, angel."

"Yes you are. You may not want to be, but you are. Guess you're gonna just have to deal with it," she giggled. "I think behind that all that badass Dom exterior, you're nothing but a big ol' cuddly bear." Pausing once more, she gazed out the window. "I haven't cuddled anyone for, well...forever."

Her voice had dropped to barely a whisper and was suffused in so much sadness it stung his heart.

"Why not?"

"Because the guy I dated when I first moved here ended up dumping me for a yoga instructor. I should have been happy. He was a jerk. He actually called me a freak because I wanted him to spank me. That's okay. I'm fine with being a freak. In fact, I'm better off without him, 'cause it never would have worked out, anyway. He was too uptight and really lousy in bed. That was a serious disappointment, I'll tell you what. He had a decent cock but had no idea how to use it."

Kellan exhaled a soft chuckle. Yeah, if she remembered any of this conversation in the morning, she'd be mortified.

"That's when I started checking out older men, like you," she continued. "I bet you have a decent cock, too. But more importantly…I bet you know *exactly* how to use it. Don't you?"

"I've never had any complaints," he managed to choke out, dreaming about all the ways he'd like to prove that to her.

"I'd be happy to rate you if you want me to," she giggled.

The air stilled in his lungs. A cold sweat broke out over his face. Mercy was trying to seduce him like some crazy reversal of Mrs. Robinson. It was killing him. He didn't know how to respond without crushing her feelings.

Fuck!

"You know, I fantasize about you all the time when I'm…well, you know, masturbating."

Don't…don't ask!

"What do you imagine me doing to you, angel?" His voice came out raspy and low.

Fucking masochist! his conscious barked.

"Everything," she purred. "Every dirty little thing I can think of."

When she let out a low, sensual moan, Kellan swallowed tightly and wrapped his hands around the steering wheel in a death grip. His cock strained against the zipper of his pants while throbbing like a tribal drum.

He needed to steer this conversation in a whole other direction, and fast.

"What kind of bed do you have?"

"Huh?" Kellan asked, wondering where her question was going to lead next.

"Your bed. What kind of bed do you have? Is it a regular mattress? I have one of those foam beds. You know, the memory kind. I need to find someone to share it with me soon, before it forgets what a man's body in it feels like."

Mercy laughed at her own joke as Kellan pulled into the driveway. He stopped at the metal gate and exhaled a heavy breath.

She stopped laughing as she stared at the two-story red brick with cut-marble accents. Her eyes grew as big as saucers. Her mouth fell slightly open. "Jesus! Is this your house?"

"Yes. Why?"

"You're not only sexy as sin but rich as Midas, too? Oh, that's so not fair."

He loved this no-holds-barred side of her. With a silent chuckle, Kellan lowered the window and punched in the code to the gate.

Mercy continued to assess his home, pressing her nose against the passenger window. "How many subs you got locked up inside there?"

"None."

"You don't live here alone, do you?"

"I do."

"Why?" She blinked. "I mean…you could house a third-world country in this…this palace."

Unable to hold it in any longer, he laughed. "It's not that big, angel."

"That's what you think. I could fit my whole apartment in one bathroom of this thing, I bet! How many bathrooms does this behemoth have in it anyway?"

"Five," he answered still grinning.

"Five! You must go through a shitload of toilet paper!"

Lord, man…why aren't you recording this on your phone?

Kellan knew why. Humiliation wasn't Mercy's thing. She yearned for a strong, steady hand, copious amounts of praise, and orgasms…lots and lots of orgasms. She was the exact kind of submissive he ached to guide, claim, and control.

After he pulled into the garage, Kellan killed the engine and gathered up the items from the hospital. "Sit tight. I'll come around the car and help you inside."

Mercy answered with a tiny nod. Frowning, she shielded her eyes from the harsh light inside the garage. Kellan knew then the shot she'd received at the hospital was starting to wear off.

He stepped from the car and adjusted his unruly hard-on, then hurried to help Mercy. As he closed the door behind her, she started to sway. Kellan wrapped his arms around her tiny waist and drew her against him. She fit his body like a glove, a fact he couldn't ignore as he led her into the kitchen.

Her sudden silence worried him. "Are you doing okay?"

"My headache's back."

Even in the dimly lit kitchen, he saw the lines furrowed between her brows. "Hang on. Let me give you some pain meds before we go upstairs."

"Thanks."

He eased her onto a padded kitchen chair at the table, then filled a glass at the sink. She thanked him again when he handed her two tablets and the water.

"I wish Mika would have gone on ahead and shot Kerr," she murmured.

"Me, too. But Officer Amblin and the rest of the Chicago PD are searching high and low for him right now. They'll find him soon and lock him up for good this time."

"I hope you're right."

"Come on. Let's get you into bed."

"Point me in the right direction and I'll take care of myself."

"No. You're going to get all loopy again in a few minutes. I don't want to find you a few hours from now passed out and drooling on the carpet."

"Why not? You've already seen me at most of my klutzier moments. What's one more going to hurt?"

"You're not a klutz. There's a lunatic after you. Big difference." He helped her rise from the chair and felt a quiver ripple through her. "Don't worry, angel. You're safe."

"For now," she mumbled.

Kellan helped her up the long, curved staircase. Mercy paused midway and turned her aqua eyes up at him. "If I haven't told you yet…thank you for helping me."

"You're welcome." He sent her a warm smile.

"God, you're handsome." Her words came out breathy, as if she'd accidently said her thoughts out loud.

"You're stunningly beautiful yourself, angel."

Kellan forced his gaze from her lips before he fucked up again and kissed her. When she stumbled on the next step, he lifted her into his arms. He'd expected her to protest, but she didn't. Mercy simply wrapped her slender arms around his neck and nuzzled her head beneath his chin.

Every step that led him closer to the bedrooms ignited a war of wills within him. Needs and wants battled it out with self-preservation and integrity. By the time he'd reached the second floor, Kellan was all but lost with her body meshed to his. He didn't know which side was winning his internal war, but at that particular moment, he didn't really give a shit.

When he reached the guest room, Kellan tore back the bedding and gently eased Mercy onto the mattress. She'd fallen sound asleep. If he felt more like a gentleman and less like a pervert, he'd remove her clothes so she could sleep more comfortably.

You're not only thinking like a pubescent teen, you're starting to act like one.

Right! No way could he leave her like this.

Memories of Hannah's bout with food poisoning three years ago crept into his brain. She'd gone with friends to check out a new Italian restaurant one night, but when she phoned him the next day, sounding like homegrown hell, Kellan raced to her apartment. He'd found his twenty-year-old daughter lying in soiled sheets, so drained of strength she couldn't muster the energy to roll over and hurl into the trashcan beside her bed. Leena was already in the nursing home, so Kellan had done what any father would do. He'd cleaned up his little girl and driven her to the hospital.

All you have to do is take care of Mercy, as you did Hannah, less the vomit.

Thankfully, he wouldn't have to strip down to his boxers and drag her into the shower with him like he'd done with Hannah. The only flaw with Kellan's theory was that Mercy didn't stir a single paternal feeling in him.

This was going to be a bitch.

Kellan mentally disconnected and focused on the clothing and not the woman as he worked the busk of the corset free. But when the material fell open, Mercy's pale breasts spilled out. Her rosy nipples drew up tight, and her silky white skin glowed in the moonlight filtering in through the window. His cock lurched eagerly against his fly, and Kellan had to stand up to keep from sliding his hands all over her smooth alabaster skin. The lump of lust lodged in his throat was all but suffocating.

Frustration spiked.

He felt like a kid with a pocket full of quarters staring at an empty gumball machine.

Cover her up and get the fuck out!

The voice in his head screamed safe, rational directions, but Kellan ignored logic. He cupped one hand on Mercy's shoulder, the other against her supple hip, and rolled her to her side. The hard peaks of her nipples grazed his thigh, and a surge of pre-come slickened his boxers. Cursing his body's spontaneous reaction, Kellan wondered why the woman made him feel so alive and young. He hadn't been this close to shooting off inside his shorts for a couple of decades.

After tugging the corset from beneath her, he released the zipper of her skirt. Easing her onto her back, he worked the clingy fabric from her hips. Mercy's tart womanly scent filled his senses. Saliva pooled in his mouth. He could all but taste the sweet cream of her pussy pouring over his tongue. His cock stretched impossibly tighter. Kellan sucked in a ragged breath and dragged the material over her legs and off her feet. He then stood and paused, taking the liberty to simply admire the gentle slope of her naked curves. The scrap of red lace that covered her bare pussy drew his gaze like a beacon. Kellan had taxed all his benevolence. He needed to get the fuck out of there. Instead, he tortured himself with one last long look at her supple flesh, full, heavy breasts, and tempting lips. A sigh, fraught with desire, escaped his lungs as he drew the covers over her sinful body, then turned and stormed down the hall.

With each irritated step, Kellan tore at his clothes. He wanted to howl like the wind with the injustice of it all. When he reached his room, he kicked out of his pants, toed off his shoes, and peeled off his sticky boxers.

His cock sprang free. Red. Angry. Leaking like a damn faucet.

Kellan clenched his jaw, wrapped a firm fist around his shaft, and flopped back onto his bed. Closing his eyes, he ruthlessly jerked his cock from stem to tip. He imagined himself in Mercy's room, spreading her supple thighs apart to bite the lacy red fabric from her slick cunt. He wouldn't dive face-first inside her beguiling pussy. No, Kellan pictured himself kissing, nipping, and laving his tongue up her shapely thighs before he buried his tongue deep inside her tight, flooded center. The sounds of her whimpers and moans filled his ears as he tongue fucked her pussy, scraping his teeth over her hard, distended clit.

He squeezed his dick in a brutal hold as he fisted himself faster and harder. Lost in the fantasy of her silken walls clutching his shaft, he envisioned filling and stretching her snug, wet tunnel. He could all but feel her bucking and writhing beneath him as she screamed his name and clenched down tight all around him.

Kellan's balls drew up tight. Tingles of demand raced down his spine. A conflagration of fire exploded behind his eyes in blinding bursts of white light.

"Aarrgghh," he growled as he pumped his cock with frenzy.

Thick ropes of hot, slick seed jettisoned into the air and splattered onto his chest. Moaning, he milked his cock dry. Spent and slightly disgusted, he sat up and grabbed his boxers off the floor, then wiped the seed sliding down his chest and abdomen.

"This is what you have Natalie for, asshole," he quietly chastised himself.

Yes, but the relief he'd achieved with her today did little to curb the hunger Mercy provoked inside him. Kellan felt zero affection for Natalie. A fact he wasn't particularly proud of, but it was the only way he could retain his mistress and live with himself. Natalie was nothing more than a placebo for his bruised and damaged soul.

But Mercy? Well, he'd already come to the vexing conclusion that she possessed the magic to heal him if he'd let her.

Kellan was quickly discovering that the more time he spent with the bold and sassy beauty the harder it became to ignore the feelings she evoked inside him. Trying to shove aside his feelings for her was like shoving a boulder up an icy mountain…impossible.

"I hate to tell you this, angel, but your big, bad-ass Dom isn't so tough after all," he groused.

Standing, he tossed his boxers in the dirty clothes basket and headed toward the bathroom. Halfway there, Kellan spied the photo of him and Leena on their wedding day. He stopped dead in his tracks.

He could still feel the warmth of her love. Still see the light that always danced in her green eyes. Taking Leena's hand in marriage had been the happiest day of his life, paling only in comparison to the birth of Hannah. The photo was a haunting reminder of the perfect life he'd lost.

Tossing a glance over his shoulder, Kellan spied the rumpled comforter on the bed. His gut twisted and a surge of oily guilt sluiced through his veins. The bed he and Leena had spent endless hours making love in was now tainted with his fantasies of another woman. Grief and shame consumed him. Tears he hadn't shed for years pricked the backs of his eyes. Kellan picked up the photo and clutched it to his chest.

"I'm sorry, Leena," he whispered. "I'm trying to stay true to you...true to our vow. But it's so damn hard. I miss you. I miss the life we shared. Miss hearing your voice...your laughter...feeling your touch. Christ, I'd give the world to feel your hands on me...on my face...my chest...my cock. I ache to hold you against me, to wake up with you beside me. Hell, I even miss our spats, because we always made up in bed, nearly busting the headboard in the process. But mostly I miss you...miss my love, my soul mate, my wife, my slave... Fuck, Leena, you were my whole goddamn world!" A tear slid down his cheek. Kellan angrily wiped it away and sucked in an uneven breath.

"The pictures...the memories, they're not enough. Not fucking nearly enough! You're supposed to be here with me, dammit! We were supposed to grow old together. But now...it's all gone. The future is empty because you're locked inside that fucking silent fortress. I can't break through to you, baby... No matter how hard I try, I can't reach you. I'll never be able to. You're gone...forever gone. I miss you, baby. Miss you so fucking bad!"

Before the claws of misery could sink inside him further and drag him down into the hell he'd spent years climbing his way out of, Kellan gently set the photo on the dresser and walked away.

He numbly adjusted the water temperature of the shower, then stepped inside the spacious pale-colored travertine walls. Positioned beneath the spray from the rainforest showerhead, Kellan tried to let the steaming water melt the grief from his flesh and cleanse the misery from his soul, but it didn't. A level of despondency he hadn't felt since Leena's accident—when he could barely drag himself out of bed—had him by the balls. Those horrific days of long ago floated through Kellan's mind. Hannah had been eighteen—a legal adult—but equally devastated. She'd needed the emotional support of her father. Kellan knew if it hadn't been for his daughter, he might still be huddled beneath the sheets of his bed, an empty, hollow wreck barely clinging to life.

His dark and dangerous stroll down memory lane was as hazardous to him as the naked sub sleeping down the hall.

Kellan raised his chin and let the thrumming water beat at the consuming loneliness.

Feeling as if he'd aged thirty years in a matter of minutes, Kellan dried and dressed in a pair of sweats and a cotton wife beater. He scrubbed a hand over his face and sucked in a deep breath, then started regaining order and control within once again.

After retrieving his cell phone from his pants that still lay bunched on the floor, Kellan sat on the edge of his bed and sent off a text to Chief Judge Jerry Tauley. He also cc'd the court clerk with his request to clear his docket for the coming week.

He knew spending the next seven days with Mercy by his side would be as painful as taking a baseball bat to his nuts. But it was the only way he could make sure she followed Brooks' orders.

"I must be the world's biggest fucking glutton for punishment," Kellan mumbled.

With cell phone in hand, he left his room and strolled down the hall. Before padding to the kitchen, he peeked in on Mercy, who was still sound asleep. He snagged a cold beer and retraced his steps to the second floor. Nearing the guest room, he heard her softly whimper. Worried that she was in pain, he entered the room to find her thrashing against the sheets. Her face was wrinkled in a tormented scowl.

Kellan sat down beside her and touched her cheek. "Wake up, angel. You're having a nightmare."

Her right fist came out of nowhere and cuffed him soundly on the chin.

"Fuck!" he roared. Pain engulfed his jaw as he lurched back and gripped his face.

Mercy's eyes flew open. She sat up and yelped. Terror was written all over her face. She quickly crab-crawled away from him until her back was pressed against the headboard. Kellan tried not to stare at her naked breasts, heaving up and down while she struggled to fill her lungs, but it wasn't happening.

"Easy, angel. It's me, Kellan. You're safe."

He forced his gaze to stay locked with hers. Seconds later, her shoulders slumped. Mercy drew in several shaky breaths as she cradled her forehead in her hand.

"I'm sorry if I woke you. I'm okay now. It was just a bad dream." Her voice sounded more sultry than usual.

"You didn't wake me, angel. Were you dreaming about Kerr…about what happened tonight?"

"I don't know…I-I don't remember now."

Kellan nodded, not wanting to prod her into resurrecting the demons who'd come to call. "You're safe here. No one is going to hurt you."

"I know. Thank you."

The need to drag his eyes from hers and skim a hungry stare over her naked flesh rode him hard. Resisting temptation, Kellan lifted the sheet and nodded for her to slide back onto the mattress.

Mercy dropped her chin and gasped. "Who… Why'd you take my clothes off?"

"So you could rest more comfortably," he replied evenly. "I've seen naked women before, angel."

"Yeah, but you haven't seen *me* naked." She scowled.

He wanted to laugh but didn't. "I didn't mean to embarrass you, but you needed to sleep without being bound in a corset. I didn't take a single indecent liberty while you were in a helpless state."

A taunting gleam shimmered in her eyes. "Helpless around you is okay. I trust you, Kellan. And if you ever decide to take any *indecent liberties* with me, just make sure I'm awake so I can enjoy it, too."

"Brat," he scolded with a chuckle. "Go back to sleep, angel. I'll wake you in a few more hours."

She nodded and slid between the sheets. "Kellan?"

"Yes?"

"Would you please stay with me until I fall asleep?"

Her voice teemed with fear, vulnerability, and a hint of shame.

Kellan aimed to piece together her shattered soul as best he could. "Close your eyes. I'll be right here."

"Thank you."

He moved her clothes to the dresser and pulled the chair up next to the bed. Within minutes, Mercy had fallen back to sleep. He finished his beer and dozed off himself. Thankfully he'd set an alarm on his phone and the vibration at four a.m. woke him. He rousted Mercy, administered more pain meds, and briefly talked until the pharmaceuticals kicked in and she drifted off once more.

So did he.

Kellan woke to sunlight spilling into the guest room. To his shock, he discovered he wasn't in the chair. No, he was *in bed* with Mercy. Her hot, naked flesh was pressed against his side.

Fuck! Fuck! Fuck!

He peered down to find she had one arm draped over his chest and her head nestled in the crook of his shoulder. His cock woke instantaneously, tenting his sweats and the sheet.

He couldn't move.

Hell, Kellan could hardly breathe.

The only woman he'd ever woken with in his arms was Leena.

Guilt bludgeoned him like a sledgehammer while flames of remorse licked up his spine. Fighting the urge to leap out of bed, Kellan began to slowly and methodically extricate himself from Mercy's deliciously warm body.

Sweat broke out over his brow when a kitten-like moan slid from the back of her throat. The erotic sound made his cock leap and the muscles of his abs grow taut.

Seven days. Seven days, fucker.

Kellan cast a scowl at his traitorous cock. The temptress would either break him or he'd be one layer shy of skinless before the week was through. A glance at his cell on the nightstand told him there was another thirty minutes before Mercy's next pain pill. If he hurried, he could jump in the shower and drop a load before she woke. Coming quickly was never a problem fantasizing about Mercy. Reaching down, he squeezed a fist around his erection, closed his eyes, and bit back a strangled groan.

"I could help you with that if you'd like me to."

His eyes flew open and as she sat up, he quickly dropped his cock. Mercy's voice was as smooth and inviting as the sheet sliding off her pale skin. Her gaze was riveted on the bulge tenting the sheet.

He swallowed tightly and sat up. "I'm sure you're more than

capable, but you're not in any shape for that. How's your head feeling this morning?"

"Better than the one between your legs, I suspect," she drawled with a playful grin.

"Yes…well, morning wood is a man's curse," he mumbled as he climbed out of bed.

Mercy dragged her eyes from his crotch, then skimmed a sensual and approving gaze up his body. Her cheeks flushed and her breathing grew shallow.

"My, my…I had no idea such rugged beauty lay beneath all those serious suits you wear," she murmured. Kellan stood there letting her drink him in. "Such wide, expansive shoulders… You really shouldn't hide those beautiful biceps, Kellan."

Mercy reached out to him, but he tensed and took a small step back.

"So you're not going to let me touch you, huh? Why? I won't break you."

Guilt.

"I didn't think you would. My reasons don't—"

"Yeah, I know." She dropped her hand and curled her lips as if something bitter lay on her tongue. "Those reasons don't concern me."

"Exactly," he bit out, unable to hide his frustration. Before tension had the chance to bloom and destroy the morning, Kellan popped out a pill from the bubble pack and held it out to Mercy.

"I really don't want any more of those. They make me loopy. Besides, my head isn't hurting that bad now." She waved his hand away. "If you give me a couple of minutes, I'll put my clothes on, and you can take me back to my car."

"You're not going anywhere, angel. You're staying right here."

CHAPTER FIVE

MERCY STRUGGLED TO KEEP from gawking at his rugged body. Sun-kissed skin—something she hadn't expected since Kellan spent his days inside a courtroom—stretched over sinewy muscles. Even his sexy tapered waist called to her in a primal carnal way.

But the mixed signals he kept sending her were driving her batshit crazy.

She couldn't touch him, but he refused to let her leave.

What the hell was that about?

His overbearing parental tone made her bristle. And the dull ache still assaulting her brain—the pain she'd lied to him about—made her feel sluggish and ill-equipped to challenge him to a test of wills.

But what disturbed Mercy the most was that his compassionate demeanor had vanished with the surrender of the moon. Last night he'd been so tender, so…well, loving. But the magic they'd shared in the dark was gone. There were no more shadows for her to hide the weak vulnerabilities pinging through her.

The daylight spilling into the room filled her with resentment.

Disappointment sank deep. A part of her wanted to yank the covers over her head and cry. Instead, she lifted her chin. Mercy was determined to leave Judge Kellan Graham's mansion, go back to her small, homey apartment, and lick her wounds in private.

"I appreciate your offer, but I can't stay here. We both have lives, jobs, responsibilities. I don't need a babysitter. I won't stay here while you play nursemaid over me like I'm some kind of invalid."

She realized her tone had been vehement and ungrateful as she watched the color drain from Kellan's face. His lips drew into a tight line before he turned his head and stared out the window. His terse expression told her he wasn't used to anyone challenging his edict, especially a sub.

Shame made her want to take back her words. After all Kellan had done for her, she'd repaid him by lashing out like an ungrateful bitch. But the hardheaded, independent woman within was irked that he'd taken it upon himself to determine her fate instead of letting her choose for herself.

Of course, if Kellan were her Dom, she'd have reacted much differently. But he wasn't; he was only a friend, a fact that sorely stung her pride.

Mercy's emotions soared and dipped like a wild roller coaster. While Kellan stared out the window, she realized she'd knocked him off-kilter. She'd never seen him like this before and wondered if he was searching for patience or if he was simply working to slide back into his well-tailored suit of aloofness.

She was now somewhat grateful for her concussion; it might be the only thing to save her lily-white ass after turning into such a shrew. Oh, but what she wouldn't give to be taken over his lap right now.

Yeah, that's not going to happen. Instead of spanking it, he'd likely kick your ass to the curb for acting like a bratty, disrespectful sub.

"You won't be working, not on your computer, and I've arranged to take a few days off to make sure you heal up as quickly as possible."

He didn't bother to look at her when he finally spoke, but the clipped, impersonal tone of his voice filled her with déjà vu. As she'd suspected, the confusing, disconnected Dom had returned.

Mercy felt sad and rejected. All the inroads they'd made…the playful banter as well as his caring compassion had vanished like a puff of smoke. Kellan had locked himself behind thick lead walls again—the ones *she* wasn't welcome to breach.

Great!

Finally, Kellan looked at her and grimly nodded. "While you shower, I'll go to the kitchen and make us some breakfast."

And he's handed down another command…priceless.

Mercy had herself to blame. She was the reason Kellan was now brooding on the dark side.

Dammit!

"A shower sounds nice. Thank you." She forced a polite smile.

He nodded and turned to leave.

Mercy had to fix this.

Ignoring her nakedness, she hurried from the bed and clutched his arm. "Wait."

He raked a gaze up and down her nearly naked body, not bothering to hide the heat and hunger dancing in his eyes.

"I'm sorry I was so rude. I didn't mean to upset you. You've gone above and beyond for me, and I-I...feel bad that I pushed you away. I'm grateful for what you're doing for me. Please...don't...close yourself off. I can't stand for that cold wall to be between us again."

He frowned.

"I'm not intentionally closing myself off, angel," he murmured in a raspy tone. "There are things I need to process that have nothing to—"

"Do with me. Yeah, yeah, I know. You keep telling me that." The side of her mouth kicked up in a quirky smile.

"Then start believing it."

He dropped his eyes and ate her up with a carnal stare.

The temperature in the room shot up a million degrees.

Tearing his gaze away, Kellan clenched his jaw and yanked the sheet off the bed before draping it over her.

"I'll leave some clean clothes for you on the dresser. After breakfast, if you feel up to it, we can run by your apartment. You can pick up whatever you need for the week."

"The *week*?" she choked out in shock. "You said a few days."

Her reaction brought a hint of a smile to his lips. Kellan shrugged. "A week *is* a few days. Go grab a shower. I'll meet you in the kitchen."

Whatever ghosts had haunted him seemed to have vanished. Mercy wanted to launch a fist into the air and cheer. She waited until he'd left the room before she spun around excitedly.

A week. A whole damn week!

Mercy had seven days to convince Kellan to be her Dom. Seven glorious nights to try and seduce him as well. The sheets tangled around her legs and she stumbled onto the bed. Pain, like blades, cut through her skull. The room swirled in a sickening roll. Her celebration came to a screeching halt as she clutched her temples and groaned.

"That was a stupid move."

When her head and stomach quieted, she sat up and untangled the sheet and entered the bathroom. Wide-eyed, she gaped at the opulence of the enormous shower, the glimmering marble floors, and gold-plated faucets.

"All this splendor and he has no one to share it with...now that's sad."

Mercy could have spent days in the lavish shower, letting the water beat the stiffness from her battered body, but Kellan was making breakfast...for *her*. She didn't intend to make him wait.

After she dried off, she discovered an assortment of toiletries on the vanity. When she'd finished in the bathroom, she found the clothes Kellan had promised sitting on the dresser. Unfolding what was clearly women's apparel, a pang of jealousy sliced deep. She'd expected him to bring her sweat pants and a tee...*his* sweatpants and tee, not something that belonged to *another* woman. But the dangling tags told her they were new...never been worn.

Where did they come from?

Who did they belong to?

And wasn't it ironic, they were her exact size?

Mercy's creeper alarm went off in a flurry of bells and buzzers.

Kellan hadn't had time to go shopping at—she looked at the tags—*Lord & Taylor* while she was in the shower. Did he keep new black Capri pants and pastel green angora sweaters lying around so the random women he brought home didn't have to take the walk of shame?

Suspicions bloomed like weeds. She'd asked him if he had a sub, not if he had a girlfriend. Dear lord...how was Kellan going to explain why she was living under his roof to a girlfriend? If Mercy were dating him, she'd kick the bitch out the door in two-point-four seconds flat.

"But he's not dating *you*. What he does or says is his problem, not yours," she mumbled while sliding on a pair of fuzzy black socks.

She left the bedroom and headed down the hall. Though she didn't know where the kitchen was exactly, a foggy memory of sitting at the table last night skipped through her brain. Following the scent of bacon, she stepped down the hall toward a walkway. Mercy peered over the banister to an open foyer below and gasped. Kellan's mansion was straight out of *Architectural Digest*.

The place was big, breathtaking, and beautiful...exactly like the man himself.

Still gaping in awe, Mercy descended the stairs. Prisms of sun reflecting from the candelabra-styled crystal chandelier above her head dotted the marble floor. On her right, by the front door, she discovered a huge office decorated in rich, masculine mahogany furniture. Leather-bound hardbacks filled the glossy bookshelves that lined two full walls. She stroked her fingertips over the edge of his wide desk and briefly closed her eyes while inhaling Kellan's familiar pheromone-filled earthy, warm scent.

Opposite his office, across the foyer, was a formal dining room. Around the large, ornately carved wooden table, Mercy counted seating for twenty-four. The enormity boggled her mind. Her stomach gurgled and she set out to find the kitchen, admiring several paintings in bright, bold, tasteful colors adorning the walls.

"Yes, if we can postpone the Gallagher trial eight or nine days, that would be perfect. Thanks, Jerry."

Lured by Kellan's voice, Mercy wound her way into the kitchen. Okay, so kitchen was too tame a word. Kellan's *cuisine galley* could put most restaurants on the Food Network to shame. Light-colored granite workspace surrounded top-end stainless steel appliances. Mercy could barely contain the urge to raid the white glossy cupboards, pull ingredients from the oversized refrigerator, and start baking something sinfully fattening. Cooking wasn't a hobby for her; it was therapy. If Mercy had ever needed therapy it was now.

When Kellan saw her in the doorway, gawking, he waved her into the room. Cell phone pressed to his ear, he pointed to the coffeepot on the counter and arched his brows. Mercy smiled and nodded. He continued discussing court cases and dates as he moved in close and pressed his body against hers, pinning her hips to the countertop. She turned a wide-eyed gaze at him over her shoulder as he reached up and took a mug from the cabinet. Enveloped in his delicious heat, a thrill raced up her spine.

He bent and pressed his face close to her neck, inhaling deeply while still talking on the phone. "Sounds good, Jerry. If there are any other conflicts, give me a call. We'll work them out."

Desire pooled low in her belly as he lifted his head but kept his imposing and decadent torso pressed against her back. Mercy had no trouble visualizing him bending her over the marble surface, instructing her to keep her arms above her head before ripping her pants down to her ankles and fucking her roughly against the counter. She swallowed down the whimper threatening to escape and tried not to spill the coffee with her trembling hands.

"Thanks, man. I'll talk to you soon."

After ending the call, Kellan inched back slightly.

"You're trembling. Are you cold, angel?" The mischievous glint that flickered in his eyes told her he was taunting her.

Oh, he wants to play games?

She was more than ready.

"No. I'm definitely not cold." Mercy peeked inside his coffee cup. "Can I warm you up?"

He tensed. In tandem, his eyes and nostrils flared.

Bingo! Her innuendo had hit its mark.

Kellan swallowed tightly and held out his mug. "Sure. I'll take a little warm-up."

"Not the kind I want to give you," she quipped with a sassy grin.

As she filled his cup, she noticed all traces of humor had left his face. Without volleying a comeback at her, Kellan turned and started cracking eggs into a large mixing bowl. Feeling a bit disgruntled and massively confused, Mercy wondered when or if she'd ever understand this complicated man. She sipped her coffee and studied him as he worked.

"Is there anything I can help you do?"

"Don't think so. I've got it all under control."

The way he liked everything…controlled, she thought with an inward smirk.

"If it were warmer outside, we could eat on the patio, but I'm afraid we'd freeze along with the food."

Following Kellan's gaze, she took in a large family room. The floor-to-ceiling windows along the back wall drew her like a moth to a flame. With coffee in hand, she meandered into the homey and inviting space. Captivated by the wooden deck and kidney-shaped swimming pool below, she drank in the forest of fir trees lining an inlaid stone path that led to the shore of Lake Michigan. The clouds on the horizon were colored in pale hues of pink, blue, and violet…as if an artist's brush had swept the sky.

"What an incredible view," she turned and called over her shoulder, startled to see that Kellan had moved in behind her.

"Isn't it?" A look of contentment lined his face. "I bought the house because of this view."

"Not the five bathrooms, huh?" Mercy softly chuckled, then stopped, suddenly confused. "Why do I think you have five bathrooms?"

A sly grin tugged his lips. "We talked about it in the car last night."

Her brows furrowed. "I don't remember that."

"It's probably best you don't." He chuckled.

"Oh, god. What did I say?"

"Nothing bad."

"Embarrassing?"

He bobbed his head from side to side with an evasive hum. "Not really."

Before she could glean any details of their mysterious conversation, he took her hand and led her back into the kitchen. After helping her into a chair, Kellan placed a plate, heaped with food, on the table in front of her.

"Is this for me or a small country?"

"It's all for you, angel."

"If you have some rule about cleaning my plate before I can leave the table, I know what I'm having for dinner."

He didn't say anything, simply stared into space with a faraway look in his eyes. A slow smile spread across his lips. He flashed her an uber-Dominant stare that made her tingle. "You know, I could modify that and make it a useful form of punishment."

Mercy giggled. "That doesn't sound very fun."

"That's why it's called punishment."

"What kind of ruckus do I have to raise before you'll take me over your knee instead?"

He pursed his lips and studied her, then turned his focus on his plate and began to eat. Silence dragged on and draped an awkward pall in the air. Even though she wanted to kick her own ass for annihilating a relatively easy conversation, Mercy was able to glean exactly where Kellan's lines had been drawn. He was hiding something…something heavy and overwhelming, but she doubted he'd ever open up enough to share the burden with her.

A part of her wanted to walk away and leave Kellan munching on bacon. Yet another part of her wanted to stand up and scream at the top of her lungs. She'd do neither. Acting out her conflicted emotions was as stupid and childish as the way she'd taunted him about spanking her. Unfortunately she didn't know how else to chip at his walls and force him to take her under his Dominant wing. Oh, well, like they said…no guts, no glory.

Slowly the tension bled away and they began talking again. While their conversation wove through the lifestyle, it skated along the periphery regarding their own D/s desires.

Stuffed to the gills, Mercy leaned back in her chair. Kellan cleared the table, returning with another pain pill in hand. Though she hated the fuzzy feeling, she relented. Her head was throbbing too harshly to refuse.

"Why don't you go rest on the couch for a bit. I'll come sit with you after I clean up the kitchen."

She nodded and swallowed the pill. Kellan helped her to the family room and onto the luxurious leather couch. He drew a soft cotton blanket over her and kissed her forehead before returning to the kitchen. Mercy listened to the clatter of dishes, silverware, and water running in the other room, feeling a bit guilty for not helping him. But soon the pills kicked in and she floated into a dark abyss.

She woke to the sound of voices somewhere far off in the house. She assumed Kellan was in his office, on the phone, but when she heard a distinct female tone, insecurities, questions, and worries pressed in around her.

Mercy pondered retreating upstairs to the guest room, but the thought of listening to Kellan and some other woman getting down and dirty in his bedroom made her want to hurl. Decidedly, she knew it was better to stay on the couch and pretend to be asleep. At least she'd save herself the agony of rejection.

You don't have time to sit around and wait for things to play out. You only have seven days!

Though her plan to charm and persuade Kellan to teach her about submission was fraught with holes, Mercy had to remove all obstacles in her way. He didn't know it yet, but he needed her as much as she needed him. If Mercy had to drive off a million women to convince him of that fact, she would.

Teeming with resolve, she sat up and tossed off the blanket. She stood and straightened both her sweater and shoulders. Striding with purpose, she homed in on the voices and determined them to be coming from Kellan's office.

Mercy entered the room expecting to find Kellan sitting behind his desk. Instead, he was sitting beside a gorgeous young blonde on a leather love seat by the window…holding her hand.

Mercy's stomach knotted.

Kellan turned as if sensing her arrival. A look of apprehension crawled across his face. His lips tightened and the blonde stopped talking in mid-sentence and looked Mercy's way before surprise lifted the other woman's brows.

Face-to-face with her competition, Mercy's bravado turned to bullshit.

Embarrassment flooded her system.

No wonder Kellan wasn't interested in her. Why would he choose a Brooks Brothers suit when he could have Armani?

Mercy felt like a fool.

"I'm sorry, I didn't mean to interrupt," she murmured. "I heard your voice and thought you were on the phone."

Liar.

The blonde smirked, her brows still poised high, and slid a sideways glance at Kellan, over to Mercy, then Kellan once more. It was as if the woman didn't know who to begin interrogating first. Her quizzical expression was replaced by a placid smile.

No doubt one she'd practiced a million times, Mercy thought wryly.

"I didn't realize you had…company. Why didn't you say something when I arrived?" the blonde asked.

Kellan's gaze sliced Mercy like a scalpel. A knowing smile tugged a corner of his mouth as he stood and motioned her into the room.

"Hannah, this is a friend of mine, Mercy O'Connor. Mercy…Hannah."

Faking a smile that should have earned her an Oscar, Mercy lifted her hand at the younger, thinner, and decidedly more innocent woman. "It's a pleasure to meet you, Hannah."

Another lie.

She quickly shook the bimbo's hand and dropped it just as fast.

"Last night, when I was out with Mika and some others, an altercation between Mercy and one of her former friends turned ugly." Kellan replayed the violent events, guarding his Dominant proclivities as well as hers and Genesis, as Hannah's perfectly waxed brows inched back up her forehead. "So, you see, Mercy will remain here while she recuperates."

Hannah flashed a sympathetic look her way. Whether the sentiment was real or manufactured, Mercy didn't know. "Oh, my god. That's terrible. Should you be up walking around?"

Nice try, bitch. You are high as Willie Nelson if you think I'm leaving this room so you can hike up your skirt and beg Kellan to fuck you over his desk. But go on. Give it your best shot. I dare you!

"Oh, I'm not bed ridden, but last night, Kellan was beyond amazing," Mercy gushed.

His eyes grew wide for a brief moment as if she'd taken a few too many pain pills.

"I bet he *was*." Hannah softly chuckled, leveling an expectant look at the man.

Mercy, too, dragged a look his way, expecting to see him flustered or at least a bit of sweat staining his brow. Instead, he wore a cocky grin.

"I don't know if I'd go so far as to call it amazing," he refuted. "Waking you up every four hours to give you pain meds wasn't what I'd call a hardship."

"I bet not." Hannah's retort dripped in sarcasm. "I'm sure you were the perfect gentleman all night long."

Yes!

The bottom-feeding bitch had taken the bait…hook, line, and sinker.

"Indeed!" he assured.

"Right." Hannah rolled her eyes. She wasn't buying his innocence for a minute.

"Ask Mercy if you don't believe me. She'll tell you the truth." He grinned.

Tell her the truth? Not on your life.

"Oh, for crying out loud," Hannah chided. "I'm not going to ask her anything, or you, for that matter. I've never thought or expected you to…turn into a monk."

"Thank goodness, because a monk I'm not," he assured with a little chuckle.

Mercy couldn't figure out why Kellan found the conversation so amusing. She expected him to be irked she was behaving like a possessive she-cat.

"Don't!" Hannah held up her hand and scowled at Kellan. "I don't need to hear another word. I love you with all my heart, but please…just stop."

Hannah's vow of love cut Mercy to the core. Like a stone, hope sank deep and fast.

"You've never delved into my personal life; I will respect your boundaries as well," Hannah continued. "Trust me. There are certain things no one wants to hear, especially any detail involving their dad's sex life."

"Dad?" Mercy choked.

Dad? What the… Oh, shit!

She gaped at Kellan. "You mean she's…Hannah is… She's your…*daughter?*"

"Of course she's my *daughter*. Who did you think she was?" The smile stretched across his face, and the knowing twinkle in his eyes all but screamed, *gotcha*!

The son of a bitch set her up!

Mercy's cheeks blazed in anger and humiliation.

The room was suddenly too small and claustrophobic.

Hannah was his *daughter*? Mercy could only imagine what the poor child was thinking…none of it good. *Child*, nothing; she and Hannah seemed close to the same age.

Which then raised the question…where was *Mrs.* Kellan Graham?

Insecurities made Mercy's stomach swirl in a slow, nauseous circle.

Submissive or not, she needed answers from Mr. Aloof and Elusive, but now wasn't the time or the place. After Hannah left, Mercy planned to grill the grin right off his face.

Bolstered by self-righteous fury, Mercy let her courage fly. One way or another, Kellan Graham was going to spill his guts, once and for all.

"Mercy? You haven't answered my question." Kellan's voice held that Dominant edge that kicked her bravery to the curb. "Who did you think Hannah was?"

Like a balloon, Mercy's conviction deflated…sputtering and swirling and landing flat on the damn floor. Kellan knew the green-eyed monster had taken a bite out of her ass…more than one, and he enjoyed the hell out of busting her…busting her like a crack whore on an episode of *Cops*.

Since the ground refused to open up and swallow her whole like she wished it would, Mercy did the only thing she could do…she pled the fifth with a silent shrug.

Kellan chuckled. "You thought Hannah was my lover, didn't you?"

"Wait...you thought...that Daddy and I were..." Hannah stammered. "Excuse me, but I think I'm going to go throw up now."

"Wait!" Mercy cried. "I'm sorry...I didn't mean... I-I. Shit!" Mercy stumbled. How was she going to dig herself out of the sinkhole that was dragging her under? "Honestly. Your dad and I are just friends, and he *really* was a perfect gentleman last night. I swear."

Changing the subject might not have been the best decision, but Mercy wanted to clear Kellan's name and clear up the misconceptions she'd planted in his daughter's head. And in doing so, if Mercy could repair her own reputation to keep Hannah from thinking her a whore, then all the better.

A smirk tugged Hannah's lips—the same one Kellan wore from time to time. "Dad's a grown man. He can do who and what he wants."

The drama was more than Mercy's damaged brain could handle. Scrubbing a hand over her forehead, she briefly closed her eyes, attempting to will the throb away. "I think it's time I lie down for a bit. Hannah, it was nice to meet you. And again, I apologize for interrupting your conversation with Kellan, and, well...for everything."

"Don't be silly," she replied. "You didn't interrupt anything important. I drop by to bug Dad every chance I get. Don't worry about the other stuff. I've recovered." She chuckled. "It was nice to meet you, too, and I hope you feel better soon."

"Thank you."

"Let me walk you up to your room." Kellan's tone held the same gentle and caring timbre from last night. Mercy's heart melted. "I'll be back in a minute, sweetheart."

"Take your time," Hannah replied.

"You really don't have to. I'm fine," Mercy protested.

"I don't want you tripping on the stairs." Kellan's firm tone was laced with warning.

Not wanting to cause an even bigger scene, she relented.

He didn't say a single word until they'd reached the guest room. When she crawled into bed, he bent and covered her. Mercy wrapped her hand around his wrist. "I'm sorry I insulted you in front of Hannah and made a fool of myself."

"You're actually worried about how your actions reflect on me, angel?"

"Of course. My stupid jealousy insulted you, Hannah, and me. I'm sorry."

He studied her for several long, silent seconds before a smile creased the corners of his mouth. "You rest now. I'll straighten things out with my daughter."

"Good luck! There's probably no way you'll ever convince her that we're not lovers after what I said. She obviously thinks you're quite the stud. Guess I'm not the only woman she's seen wandering into your study early on a Saturday morning."

"Pull in your claws, angel. Your jealousy's caused enough trouble for one day."

"I know," she grumbled. "I just thought that...if Hannah isn't the reason you won't teach me about the lifestyle, then maybe there's another gorgeous woman who is that reason."

"No." He answered.

"Again with the one-word answers. Lovely," Mercy mumbled under her breath. "Will you at least tell me why? I want to be a better submissive. Is that such a crime? I'm not asking you to date me or get engaged... Hell, I'm not even asking you to collar me."

"I'll think about it. Now get some rest."

"Think about which part?" Mercy pressed. "Actually training me, or telling me why you won't?"

"Both."

"Arg!" she growled. "You are the most infuriating man on the planet, you know that? Getting a straight answer from you is like trying to piss up a rope. It's impossible."

Kellan grinned. "And training you would be like trying to tame a man-eating tiger."

"I can be submissive, dammit!"

His grin widened.

Damn, he's sexy.

Mercy silently barked for her wayward hormones to shut the hell up.

"Then prove it," Kellan dared.

"Fine. Challenge accepted. I'll show you that I can be the best submissive on the whole damn planet," she huffed in a purely un-submissive tone.

Kellan laughed so deep and rich that goose bumps pebbled her arms. Her nipples grew tight. The restless, sexually deprived woman inside roared to life.

"You're going to have to try much harder than that, angel."

Yes, Mercy knew that. And the sooner she was better, the sooner she could show him she was worthy of his training and his trust.

"I *will* prove that I'm submissive and not the man-eating tiger you think I am, Kellan…er, Sir."

"I look forward to that." A flash of desire darkened his eyes before he pressed a tender kiss to her forehead. "Sleep, angel."

"Yes, Sir." She closed her eyes and listened as his footfalls faded down the hall.

A satisfied smile crept along her lips. Mercy couldn't wait to show him all the desires yearning to break free from inside her. She'd start as soon as she got some sleep so her annoying headache would go away.

Naked, Mercy knelt on the thick carpet. Kellan stood in front of her…silent as usual. With her eyes cast toward the floor, she studied the laces of his polished black dress shoes in her peripheral vision. He had one strong hand cinched tight in her hair, sending prickles of glorious pain skittering over her scalp. A shiver enveloped her when he traced the outline of her jaw with the tip of his finger.

"You…on your knees, ready to please is such a pretty picture, angel," Kellan whispered. His voice teemed with pride. "You do want to please me, don't you?"

"More than anything, Sir."

Peace and serenity filled her.

"Stand, slut!"

Without warning his voice turned angry and impatient. Something was wrong. She'd screwed up somehow. Mercy hopped to her feet, trembling in fear. When he gripped her chin, pinching the flesh between his fingers and thumb, she bit back a yell.

"Look at me when I talk to you, bitch!" Kellan snarled.

No. No. This wasn't right. He wasn't right. Something was wrong with him. He'd never made her feel afraid before.

"Are you deaf, cow?" he spat. "Apologize!"

"I'm sorry, Sir." *Though she had no idea what she was sorry for, the response rolled off her tongue.*

"Prove it. Bend over the bed." His face contorted in rage. When Mercy hesitated, an evil smile crawled across his mouth. "You're not a submissive at all, are you?"

"I am, Sir. I am."

"Stop wasting my time and show me. Make me believe you want to please me."

He released her hair and was suddenly holding a long leather crop. Mercy trembled. She hated the crop.

"You'll take every lash without making a sound, or I'll beat you bloody."

He ignored her whimper of fear and narrowed his eyes.

"Why are you acting like this with me?"

Kellan raised his hand and slapped her hard across the face. White-hot pain enveloped her flesh. She pressed her lips together, holding back a scream. She didn't want to anger him any further especially when she saw a fiery satisfaction flickering in his eyes.

"Who do you think you are to question me, you stupid cunt? I'm going to enjoy punishing you for that."

The sound of his icy laughter echoed in her head. As if he suddenly possessed superhuman strength, Kellan shoved her face-first onto the bed. Mercy's throbbing cheek lay against the scratchy surface of the comforter as silent tears spilled onto the fabric.

"Are you crying for me? Aw, thank you, slut. You remembered how much I love hearing you cry, didn't you, Symoné? You remember all the wicked things I like to do to you, right?"

Mercy's heart felt as if it were going to explode from her chest. She knew that voice. It wasn't Kellan's. It was Kerr's. Terror seized her. Mercy struggled, but she found the courage to raise her head and peer over her shoulder. Kellan was still standing there. Her brain was warped in confusion and fear. Mercy knew in her heart he would never do anything as vile and brutal as this to her. She was sure Kerr had spoken to her. But he wasn't there…only Kellan.

"What's wrong, bitch? Having trouble trying to wrap your head around it all?" The sound of Kerr's evil laughter tore from Kellan's mouth. "Maybe this will help you figure it out, you ignorant bitch."

Kellan reached up started tearing the flesh off his face. The shock of seeing chunks of skin fall away sent a wave of nausea through her. Mercy gagged on the bile that burned the back of her throat. She wanted to scream…wanted to squeeze her eyes shut, but she couldn't.

"I took care of your boyfriend. How else did you think I cut his face off and covered my own with it?"

As Kerr ripped the last piece of flesh and dropped it on the floor, he smiled at her. It was the same terrifying, maniacal grin he'd worn at the courthouse and outside the club.

"I told you I'd be back to drain the life out of you, didn't I, bitch?" he taunted in a chilling tone. "Well, here I am. I always keep a promise."

He shoved his knee into her back, holding her in place before he waved a huge sharp knife in her face.

"First, I'm going to fuck your nasty cunt and asshole, then I'm going to start cutting…cutting pieces of your fucking body off and laying them right here on the bed so you can see exactly what I'm doing." Kerr patted the mattress near her face.

She was going to die a slow and painful death.

Seized with fear, Mercy screamed at the top of her lungs.

CHAPTER SIX

AFTER KISSING HANNAH good-bye, Kellan climbed the stairs to check on Mercy. Relieved to find her asleep and resting her brain, he knew he should have turned and left the room, but his feet…hell, his whole body refused to cooperate. Instead, he eased into the chair beside the bed and drank in her peaceful, delicate features. A smile tugged his lips as he remembered how adorable she'd looked in his study…jealous as hell and twice as sassy.

Her reaction had been quite a boost to his old ego. Of course, if he'd been half a gentleman, Kellan would have introduced Hannah as his daughter from the very start. But he had a sadistic bastard inside him from time to time and was curious to see just how far Mercy would go.

His smile faltered.

Hannah's visit would prompt a million questions from Mercy, none of which he was ready to answer, at least not yet. Oh, Kellan knew he'd eventually have to come clean about Leena, sooner or later, but he wanted to learn more about Mercy. She might be sympathetic to his moral dilemma, but he worried she might be sickened at the thought of…

Of what? Staying friends, or do you think you could actually offer her something more, like…commitment?

He exhaled a heavy sigh. He knew the answer. But as Hannah had reminded him earlier, life wasn't always black and white. If he found the strength to grow a pair and managed to keep his hands off Mercy sexually, he might possibly be able to teach her about the lifestyle. But eventually she'd grow tired of simply scening with him. She'd beg for his collar, and when he was forced to refuse, it would crush her. He couldn't claim her as his slave. Couldn't promise the kind of commitment he craved to give her…the one she, too, craved and deserved. Because in his heart, he was still Leena's Master.

Kellan scrubbed his hands over his face.

Contemplating anything so foolish was a waste of time.

He and Mercy could share a friendship, but that was all.

She'd already burrowed too deeply inside him.

Fuck! He couldn't even walk past the damn guest room without waltzing inside to stare at her enticing beauty.

She weakened him…his resolve…his emotions.

The power she wielded over him was frustrating. He'd never allowed himself to be so susceptible to any woman other than Leena. Kellan didn't know how to cope with his own weakness…the weakness Mercy made him feel.

The conversation he'd had with Hannah in his study earlier wormed its way into his brain.

He'd explained to his daughter that he wasn't sexually involved with Mercy. Of course, he hadn't confessed that he damn well wanted to be. But his daughter wasn't buying it, at least not in the beginning.

"Just friends?" Hannah had scoffed. "Daddy, please. I'm not three years old anymore. I know Santa Clause and the Easter bunny don't exist. Stop, please! I see the way you look at her…the way Mercy looks at you."

"That's not the point," Kellan argued. "I'm married."

"To a zombie." Pain pinched her features. "I'm sorry, but it's true. Mom left us a long time ago, and you stopped living, Dad. I've watched you. Mom wouldn't want that. She'd want you to be happy."

"I am happy. I have you."

"I'm your daughter. I'm talking about companionship…love. Don't lock your heart away in the same prison that's holding Mom." Hannah frowned. "Does Mercy know about her yet?"

"No. And I intend to keep it that way."

Hannah shook her head, wearing an expression that screamed he was being obtuse.

"You and Mercy obviously have feelings for one another. Act on them, Dad. You only live once." Her voice dropped to a whisper. "None of us are promised a tomorrow."

"I'm not going to commit adultery, Hannah."

"You already are. Natalie. Remember?"

Her words rocked the foundation out from under him. Kellan had no clue Hannah knew about his mistress.

"How did you know?"

Hannah gave him a dismissive wave of her hand. "Last summer, you were out cleaning the pool. When I came inside to get us some drinks, the phone was ringing. I didn't get to it in time and the answering machine picked up. A woman left a message reminding you it was time to renew the contract for Natalie's apartment. I quickly put two and two together."

"I'm sorry you found out."

"I'm not." Hannah scoffed. "Are you in love with both of them...Natalie and Mercy?"

"No. Natalie and I have no emotional ties whatsoever. It's nothing but... No. I don't love her."

"But you do Mercy. I see it...feel it. Don't you see, you're already committing adultery, Dad...at least adultery of the heart. If you're afraid I'm going to think less of you for loving someone other than Mom, you're wrong." Hannah paused and studied him. "That's not what you're afraid of, is it? No, you're afraid that because you have feelings for Mercy... that you're being unfaithful to Mom. That's it, isn't it?"

Kellan stared at his daughter. She was too observant and way too smart. "I took a vow to her, before God and a whole roomful of people."

"She took a vow to you, too, Daddy. But either God or Satan or fate playing a sick and cruel joke on us annulled it." Hannah quickly swiped a tear from her cheek. "She'd want you to be happy, Daddy. She loved you enough to want you to go on without her."

He couldn't find the courage to tell his daughter that he'd foolishly clung to the hope that one day Leena would wake from her catatonic prison. That she could come home once again, and they'd spend the rest of their lives happy and hopelessly in love...like some fucking storybook.

Kellan swallowed the ball of emotion lodged in his throat and hugged his daughter fiercely. "I'll think about it, sunshine," he choked.

"I love you, Daddy. You're my whole world. I want you to be happy again. It's not healthy living alone and isolating yourself the way you do. Like you and Mom always taught me...life isn't black and white; it's a million shades of gray. Let yourself love again, fully and completely. It's time to move on. Really, it is."

Mercy stirred in her sleep, drawing Kellan back to the present.

Hannah was right. He could easily lose his heart to Mercy. Hell, in many ways, he already had. But could he live with himself? The jury was still deliberating that one. Of course, there was always the chance that once she learned he was legally still married, she'd loathe him. Mercy possessed a strong moral fiber. He'd seen her display it time and time again at Genesis.

What a goddamn clusterfuck!

"No. No." Mercy's whimper was filled with fear.

Moving in close to her, Kellan watched as her tears spilled onto the pillow.

Fucking Kerr. The prick was still tormenting her dreams.

A long, mournful wail tore from her throat. Kellan couldn't allow her to suffer through another nightmare. Gripping Mercy's arm to keep her from clubbing him in the jaw again, he shook her gently.

"Wake up, Mercy," he commanded in a tone he only used at the club.

She bolted upright, nearly head-butting him, and let out a loud, long, blood-curdling scream. Her eyes wildly searched the room, no doubt looking for the son of a bitch Kerr.

"Mercy!" he repeated in the same firm tone. "You're safe. See? No monsters here…just me."

Her eyes grew wide and her face paled. "Get away from me. Don't touch me!"

The fierceness of her growl and bared teeth told him this wasn't the same nightmare she'd experienced last night. Kellan raised his hands in surrender and inched back into the chair. "It must have been a pretty bad one this time."

Mercy drew her knees to her chest, wrapped her arms around her legs, and nodded.

"Purge it from your mind and tell me about it."

Her chin began to quiver and fat tears slid down her cheeks.

It gutted him to see her so lost, broken, and frightened. The distance he'd purposely put between them to soothe her gnawed him up inside. He needed to comfort her…soothe her and vanquish the terror in her eyes. Slowly, Kellan eased onto the bed. She shot him a sideways look of warning but didn't stop him.

"Relax and take a deep breath. You know I'd never do anything to hurt you, right?"

She looked to be weighing his words carefully. After several long seconds, Mercy finally nodded, then let out a mournful wail as she launched herself into his arms.

Relief flooded his system and he engulfed her tiny frame tightly. He hugged her to his chest and let her sob. Whatever terrifying scene had unraveled in her brain, it had clearly sent her over the edge far more than her actual assault.

"Shh, it's okay, angel. I've got you. No one's going to hurt you while I'm around."

"It *was* you, at least in the beginning," she choked out.

"Me? What did I do? Tell me."

"You... I-I was on my knees for you, and you wanted me to please you."

What she began describing wasn't terrifying at all. In fact, it was one of his favorite fantasies...her on her knees before him. But he knew something more ominous was coming.

"My heart was soaring. I was so ready to show you how..." She paused as a mighty tremor shook her body. "But then you turned mean and started treating me like K-Kerr. I was scared. When I told you that I didn't understand, you got even more pissed and started ripping your face off."

Okay, so he hadn't been expecting anything quite so gory. Kellan squeezed her tight, silently offering encouragement for her to continue.

"But then, Kerr said that he killed you and was wearing your face as a mask. I think he wanted to confuse me, but it wasn't you...it was him. He told me..." She sobbed harder. "He repeated what he told me last night."

"What did he say to you last night?"

Mercy didn't answer. She sucked in several deep breaths, as if trying to regain her composure. Kellan waited patiently for her to answer him.

"He said he'd be back to drain the life out of me."

The palpable wave of fear that rolled off her nearly flattened Kellan.

Kerr's continued reign of terror over Mercy made him want to punch his fist through the fucking headboard. Kellan couldn't speak. He was too busy biting back his fury as he gently stroked his hand up and down her arm.

"It was so real," she whispered. "H-He pulled out this huge knife and told me that he was going to cut me into pieces and lay them out on the bed for me to see."

Mercy inched back. She raised her red-rimmed eyes up at him and Kellan's heart squeezed. He wiped her tears with the pads of his thumbs and pressed a soft kiss to her forehead.

"I'm scared." Her confession was whispered so softly he almost didn't hear it.

Seeing this feisty, self-assured woman reduced to a shattered shell of terror made his blood boil. The primal need to protect her and slay her fears consumed him. Though stupid and dangerous, Kellan couldn't help himself; he cupped her cheeks and brushed a featherlight kiss over her lips.

Mercy mewled. She hesitated for one brief second and then melted against him.

Her surrender set his whole world on fire.

Cinching a fist in her silky hair, Kellan guided her head back as he palmed her slender neck. When he stroked his tongue over her petal-soft lips, Mercy instantly parted them, welcoming him inside her mouth. Plunging deep, he swept his tongue over every wet, silky crevice.

Liquid silver shot through his veins.

The kiss turned raw and demanding.

His cock lurched.

Mercy dragged her fingertips up his arm, leaving a trail of sputtering electricity against his skin.

His eager shaft grew harder, hungry to squeeze inside her hot, slick openings, and claim her heart, mind, body, and soul.

His pulse thundered and roared in his ears.

Mercy clutched his shoulders, hanging on for dear life, while their tongues swirled and explored in a sultry, wet dance.

She rocked her hips as she ardently meshed herself against him.

She was so fucking responsive, so alive.

He felt as if she'd awakened him from a century-old slumber.

Molded perfectly to him, her lips...hell, her whole body felt soft, like warm velvet.

Kellan's head swam.

He was lost.

He couldn't devour her fast enough.

Couldn't slake the ruthless hunger she unleashed inside him.

Couldn't keep from touching her silky, hot flesh.

Kellan inched a hand under her sweater. The sensual heat of her body instantly enveloped him. He scraped his thumb over her bra. The feel of her pebbled nipple sent a guttural growl to roll up from his chest. Mercy answered with a needy tone of her own, then arched her back, pressing her heavy breast into his palm.

The sultry little siren was sending him up in flames.

Eating at her like a man possessed, Kellan kneaded and squeezed her supple orb.

He was gone…lost in the raging fire of sweet Mercy.

She started tugging at his tee, lifting it up over his abs and to his chest. He felt her frustration as she struggled to peel it off his body. He broke from her mouth long enough to shuck the material over his head. When he bent to claim her lips, she was gazing with awe at the definition of the muscles etched on his abs. For once, all the hours of sweating and straining at the gym had paid off.

He deftly grabbed the hem of her sweater, pulled it from her body, and sent it sailing over the side of the bed. While he gazed at the swell of her milky-white breasts protruding from beneath the bronze-colored bra, Mercy placed her palms on his chest and dragged them down his torso.

His body hummed and his mouth watered.

When she reached behind her back and began working the clasp of her bra, reality hijacked Kellan's libido.

What the fuck are you doing? She has a concussion! Remember? She's not well enough for all the things you want to do to her. You're supposed to be a responsible Dominant. Start acting like one!

His subconscious' smack upside the head caused the fog of lust to vanish.

Kellan blinked at Mercy. Still mesmerized by the sight of her half-naked body and swollen, wet lips, he wondered how he'd allowed things to get so far out of hand so damn quickly.

Fuck!

He had to put the brakes on…fast.

"No. Wait. Don't do that."

Mercy stilled. Her brows furrowed.

"Your brain needs time to... You're not well enough for us to do this."

"I'm fine. If you think you're stopping now...I'll give *you* a concussion, mister."

While he wanted to laugh at her threat, he'd much rather have taken the sassy hellcat over his knee and set her ass on fire. Kellan couldn't stand it when subs tried to Top from the bottom. Ever since finding her in his courtroom yesterday, Mercy had been consciously or subconsciously trying to manipulate him. Did she even know her behavior was unacceptable for a sub? Kerr probably never bothered to teach her about protocol at all.

She needed education and enlightenment.

Needed a firm, guiding hand.

Needed *him*.

Kellan wasn't ready to shove a stake in the ground quite yet. He needed time to decide if he could actually move on and live happily ever after as Hannah had urged him to do.

Oh, so training this eager sub is suddenly outside your wheelhouse, but stripping her bare and fucking her injured brains out is perfectly fine? Stop screwing with her head. Get your shit together, ace!

Before Kellan could retrieve her sweater and cover up the creamy temptation of flesh, the straps of her bra slid down her arms. The molded cups followed next until she was left wearing nothing but the black pants.

He mutely stared at her breasts. Her rosy-pink nipples drew up before his eyes. He wanted to pluck and suck her succulent berries. Kellan's heart and cock lurched in tandem. Like a rolling blackout, the synapses in his brain began shutting down. All energy was redirected to his cock, now growing impossibly tighter.

With a look of determination lining her face, Mercy clasped his wrist and drew his hand to one soft, plump, and pear-shaped breast.

Oh, this was going way beyond Topping from the bottom.

Submitting to her did not bode well.

Time to take control of the feisty, usurping sub.

Kellan jerked his had free and pinned her with a warning glare.

"What do you think you're doing, angel?" His reprimand was low and even. Mercy blinked up at him as a crimson hue painted her cheeks. "You're not in charge, little one. I'm the Dom. You're not allowed to control me in any fashion, ever again. Is that clear?"

As he laid down the law, he softly stroked a knuckle over the fiery flesh of her face.

His erection throbbed like a virgin heart and strained beneath his sweats like a goddamn flagpole. Ignoring his body's incessant demand, Kellan bent and retrieved her sweater from the floor and handed it to her.

"Put this back on."

A single tear slid down her cheek as she wordlessly complied.

"Look at me, Mercy."

She closed her eyes briefly and sucked in a deep breath, then raised her chin. She met his gaze. Beneath her unshed tears, Kellan saw a cyclone of emotions swirling inside her: shame, regret, confusion, and desire were the most prevalent.

She was so fucking lost.

He couldn't *not* help her.

Kellan squared his shoulders, clasped his hands behind his back, and welcomed the slide into the glorious peace and freedom of total Dominant headspace.

"Hands behind your head, angel." He purposely lowered his voice while infusing his tenor with what Mercy needed: command, control, and direction.

A tremor shook her body as she sucked in a startled breath. Kneeling up on the bed, she raised her arms and clasped her fingers behind her head before lowering her lashes, in total submission.

He let loose an inward roar.

His pulsating cock leaked like a sieve.

He'd lost count of the number of times he'd fantasized seeing here before him in this way. Like in his dreams, her sublime surrender made him want to gorge on her…fill the empty places inside him with her power, her precious trust. His palms itched to cup her proffered breasts and absorb her yielding energy…let it flow through him and feed the emaciated Dominant inside him.

It was a heady rush knowing that with one simple command, Mercy would willingly hand everything over to him, her power, her passion, her love.

She would beg him to wrap his lips around her pebbled nipples, flick and lave his tongue over her crinkled flesh. Whimper and moan for him as he feasted on one, then the other before tearing her pants down over her hips. He'd direct her to spread her bare, wet folds open and inhale the spicy sent of her cunt, then devour her until she was ready to shatter. Kellan would warn her not to come, and she'd follow his command. Not out of fear but out of the need to please him. And when he hoisted her legs over his shoulders and drove his dripping cock deep inside her quivering core, she'd whisper to him...tell him that she loved him.

"I want to touch you so badly, Sir," Mercy whispered without raising her head.

Kellan briefly closed his eyes to will away the carnal fantasy uncoiling in his head.

Rescue her with your control and command.

"As I do you, angel. But we can't always have what we want."

"I know, Sir."

"And I hate to tell you this, little one, but you won't ever have what you want if you continue to Top from the bottom. Do you know what that means?"

"Trying to get my own way?"

"Yes, by trying to manipulate a Dom."

"I would never do that."

"You already have, numerous times."

She raised her lids and gaped at him as if he were from Mars. "When?"

It took all the self-control he could muster not to grin. She was so fucking precious...so intriguingly innocent in the ways of submission.

"Do you actually want me to list them all?"

"Yes."

"Yes what?"

"Yes, please."

"Yes, please *who*?"

"Oh. Yes, please, Sir."

"Very well. We'll start at the top. In my chambers yesterday, you argued with me when I informed you that I would take you home."

"But...but you weren't Dominating me then."

"Wasn't I? My Dominance isn't a switch, little one. It doesn't flip on and off like a light bulb. While I can adjust it at will, make no mistake, even when I'm lenient, I'm man and Dom...one entity."

"Oh," she whispered. Her lips remained pursed in an inviting O. Christ, he wanted to kiss her again.

"In the parking garage. You handed down the ultimatum if I didn't answer your question. Do you remember?"

"Yes, Sir," she replied. Her quiet reply was teemed in remorse.

She was finally beginning to understand. Her awakening filled him with pride.

"Shall I continue?"

"No, Sir. I get it."

"Do you?"

She nodded, though a bit too pensively for his liking.

"Tell me then, think back…what do you suppose was your boldest attempt to usurp my Dominance?"

"They all seem pretty foolishly bold at the moment."

"Attempting to blindly find your way is anything but stupid. It takes guts to try and spread your submissive wings without someone there to show you how to fly." He paused and let her ponder his words. "I'll help you figure out the answer. It was just now, when you disobeyed me and removed your bra after I instructed you not to."

"I-I…" Her rebuttal died on her lips as he sent her a frown. She lowered her gaze again. "I thought you didn't want me…sexually."

Kellan placed his fingers beneath her chin and lifted her head until she met his eyes once more. "Nothing could be further from the truth. I've wanted you since the first night I laid eyes on you. There's nothing I want more than to release my cock, grip your silky hair, and drag your mouth to me. Feel your slender fingers slide over my rigid shaft as you part your pretty, plump lips and glide your hot, slick tongue all over me."

Her whole body trembled. Mercy sucked in a raspy breath. Heat danced in her shimmering aqua eyes. "I'd like that, too, Sir."

Kellan was in awe of the girl.

She possessed the heart of a true submissive. While that heart had led her to hook up with Kerr and brought a world of shit down around her, she hadn't broken. Her spirit, her desire, her need to yield and please had survived. Mercy possessed the same brave, sassy spunk that Leena once had.

But it had taken the courage to exert his Dominance, boldly put Mercy on her knees here before him, to realize how he'd missed someone who challenged him the way she did.

"Unfortunately, we can't. I know from experience that concussions don't heal overnight. It's my duty as a Dom to protect you in all ways—physically, emotionally, and mentally."

"Mild concussion," she corrected, then quickly bit her lips together as if she'd screwed up.

"Let's get one thing straight. I don't ever want you to conceal your feelings. You're free to always speak your mind, but Topping from the bottom won't be tolerated. Understood?"

"Yes. Thank you. I was afraid I'd be wearing a permanent ball gag if I couldn't express myself."

Kellan chuckled. "You don't like ball gags?"

"I hate them."

"I'll be sure to remember that." He grinned.

"I bet you will." She bit back a taunting smirk. "But I am feeling better."

"I'm glad to hear that, but you're still not well enough for… Well, let's just say your physical health supersedes everything for now."

"Yes, Sir."

Her reply was no different than all the other subs at the club, but when those two words rolled off Mercy's lips, his Dominance expanded along with his chest and his cock. Kellan could feel her trust. He could easily see himself gathering up the intricate pieces of her submission and sculpting her precious power into a mind-shattering new world for her. Their shared pleasures would be more than immense.

The image of watching her soar to the heavens under his command unleashed a sizzle of want to sear his balls. Clutching his hands tightly to keep from losing his shit and touching her, Kellan bent and kissed her forehead.

"You may lower your arms now, angel."

"Thank you, Sir."

Her breathless reply taunted his angry erection. In a perfect world, he'd lift her off the bed and carry her down the hall. He'd strip her naked and put her on her knees in his shower and fill her mouth with every hard inch of him.

But this wasn't a perfect world…it was a perfect storm, named Mercy. And Kellan was caught in the eye.

"Relax and rest some more if you can. I'm going to grab a quick shower." *And jack off again, 'cause who doesn't need a chapped dick? Dammit!* "In a little bit, we'll drive to your apartment and pick up your things."

"Thank you for everything...Sir."

"You're welcome."

Her gratitude warmed him all the way to the shower and through another quick but powerful orgasm courtesy of his fist. As Kellan stood at the dresser fastening the button of his jeans, he gazed at the wedding photo once again.

"I don't know if I can move on yet or not, love. Hannah's convinced you'd want me to," he whispered. "It's the guilt that's living, breathing inside me I'm not sure I can overcome."

Confessing his fears, even to Leena's image, seemed to lighten some of the load from his shoulders. If he knew for certain that she would want him to forge ahead, his decision would be a no brainer. He'd not only train Mercy, but collar her, and move her in with him as well.

"No one ever said life was fair or easy," he grumbled before choosing a shirt from the closet.

Dark, ominous clouds drifted overhead as he and Mercy drove to her apartment.

"I'll try to be quick so we don't end up like a couple of drowned rats on the drive back to your place."

"Take your time. A little water won't hurt us." Kellan grinned. "Do you have your keys?"

"No. I have a spare under the mat."

He arched his brows in shock. "That's probably not a wise thing to do, especially with Kerr still on the lose."

"You're right. I shouldn't leave a key there. They haven't caught him yet?"

"No. Before Hannah arrived, I phoned Amblin. He's as frustrated as we are. Kerr seems to have vanished off the face of the earth."

Mercy nibbled her bottom lip as worry stamped her features.

Kellan reached over and clasped her hand. "I'll keep you safe. Trust me."

"I do trust you and I know you'll do everything in your power to keep him from me."

"Damn straight."

As he pulled in and parked in front of her complex and turned off the ignition, Mercy eyed the empty slot where she normally parked. "Oh, I just realized...my car's still at the club. Crap. I have no idea where the key is. I had it before..."

Kellan raised his hand. "Relax. Everything's fine. I, ah, I'm sorry, I forgot to tell you. Things were a bit hectic last night. Your car and key are safe and sound. Mika texted me while we were at the hospital. After things settled down at the club, Woody went outside to make sure your car was locked and found your key lying on the street. He took it inside and gave it to Mika. Max or maybe Samantha drove it to Mika's after Genesis closed to make sure it didn't get towed," Kellan explained while watching the anxiety bleed from her face. "When you're able to drive, we'll go over to Mika's place and pick it up."

"I can't believe this."

"What?"

"Everyone at the club...they've opened their hearts to me. I have no idea how I'll ever be able to repay them...and you."

"You don't have to. We're a close-knit, kinky family. We take care of our own." Far off in the distance, a flash of lightning webbed the sky. "We'd better get inside. I don't want you to be melting."

At least not in the rain.

Kellan preferred her to melt all around him. Before his unruly cock woke again, he hurried from the car and helped Mercy into the complex. He bent and lifted the rubber welcome mat outside her apartment door. A loud clap of thunder shook the building just as Mercy touched his shoulder.

"Wait. It's been moved."

"What?"

"The key. I never place it sideways...always vertical."

Kellan plucked up the key and stood. "Wait over there until I check things out."

"What if he's in there, waiting for me? You might get shot."

He bent and lifted the leg of his jeans, then lifted the Glock G28 from the holder strapped to his ankle. While this model was only assigned to law enforcement officers, most of the judges were granted licenses for them, just in case things went south during a trial.

"You have a gun?" Mercy's eyes widened.

"I usually only carry it for work, but after last night, I won't be leaving home without it."

She gave a tiny nod before walking toward the entrance near her door.

"I'll be out in a minute." He gave her a wink as he slid the key into the lock.

Kellan stepped inside and flipped on the light.

The words: YOU'RE GOING TO DIE, BITCH were painted on the wall above her couch.

His gut and jaw clench simultaneously.

A flash of lightning illuminated the ominous message. The hairs on the back of his neck tingled. Though he wanted to inspect the rest of the rooms, Kellan knew he needed to preserve the crime scene. Frustration ate at him as he eased out of the apartment and let the door close in his face.

"What's wrong? Why did you come out so fast?" Mercy nervously asked as she hurried in beside him.

Kellan gripped her elbow and led her to the stairwell leading up to the second floor and nodded for her to sit down. Rain pounded against the glass panels framing the main door. Thunder and lightning added to the sense of foreboding that clung to his flesh.

"You're scaring me. What did you see that made you leave so fast? Was Kerr there?"

As Kellan scanned the entryway, he pulled out his cell phone. "Give me a minute and I'll answer you."

As he dialed 911, Mercy gasped and covered her mouth with a trembling hand.

"This is Judge Kellan Graham," he stated to the operator. "I need to report a 549."

"In progress?" she asked.

"I don't believe the perp is still at the location, but I'm not sure. You need to let Officer Amblin know I've called this in. I have reason to believe this is connected to one of his ongoing investigations."

After relaying Mercy's address to the dispatcher, Kellan hung up the phone and sat down beside her. Placing his gun on the step next to him, he wrapped Mercy in his arms while they silently watched the storm rage outside.

He was thankful as fuck that Mercy was now staying with him. Images of what could have happened if she'd returned to her apartment alone last night spooled through his head.

Kellan knew she'd be horrified by what lay waiting inside, but there was nothing he could do or say to candy-coat Kerr's ghastly threat. All Kellan could do was try and cushion the blow. While he hoped the vile message would be the extent of the damage, deep down he feared it was but the tip of the iceberg.

"I think Kerr found the key you left under the mat. He, or someone has been inside your apartment."

"Why? How do you know?"

"There's something ugly spray-painted on the wall above your couch."

"That motherfucker! Did you look in my office? Is my gun...my computer... Oh, god. My whole life is on that thing. If he..."

When she tried to stand, Kellan held her firmly in place, feeling the panic that consumed her. "I don't know. When I saw the shit on the wall, I stepped back out."

"We have to look. I need to see if he stole my computer...my jewelry... Why are we just sitting here?" Terror strained her voice as tears filled her eyes.

"Because that's what we *need* to do. We can't go inside. We might inadvertently mess up the crime scene. If we touch something that held the only fingerprint he left behind, we'd ruin the only chance we might have of adding more time to Kerr's, or whoever's sentence."

"Why do you keep saying *or someone or whomever*? We both know it was Kerr who broke in." She rested her elbows on her knees and cupped her face in her hands.

"Occupational hazard, I guess. You know...the whole innocent-until-proven-guilty thing?" He shrugged.

"What vulgar words did that bastard paint on my wall? No. Wait. Let me guess...bitch, whore, slut, right?"

"No. It was a threat, angel."

"Tell me what it says. Please!"

Kellan exhaled a heavy sigh and scowled. "It said, 'You're going to die, bitch.'"

CHAPTER SEVEN

STRUGGLING TO KEEP from succumbing to the panic rising inside her, Mercy pressed a palm to her swirling stomach and gritted her teeth. In the past, she might have naïvely let Kerr violate her body, but he didn't have permission to invade and vandalize her home, her sanctuary, and trash all she'd worked hard to achieve. She wanted to hunt him down and beat him to death...put an end to his reign of terror.

Feeling as if she were crawling out of her skin, Mercy shoved at Kellan to get him off her.

"What are you—"

"I know you're trying to comfort me, and I'm grateful...honestly. But I feel like I'm suffocating. I need to get up...pace...work off some of this anger before I explode."

Kellan chuckled softly and released her.

"What's so damn funny?" She lurched to her feet.

"Nothing. I thought you might fall apart over all this, but I can see now that I was wrong. You're ready to kick ass."

"Damn straight. That...that...prick has no right to torment me or all the other shit he's doing," she railed. "He's crazy. Certifiably insane. Off his fucking rocker. And he picked the wrong woman to fuck with. If I have to, I will hunt him down and make him wish he were never born."

"Settle down, Wonder Woman, you won't be going anywhere without me by your side and until your head has healed. But I'll make you a promise. If Kerr happens to come strolling in the door, I'll hand you my gun and you can blow his head off."

"Perfect! I'll aim for the little worthless head in his pants first...then finish him off after he's suffered enough. I think a week or two ought to do it," she growled.

"Remind me never to piss you off, angel."

The sexy crooked grin on Kellan's face took some of the starch out of her, but the storm inside raged in time with the one wreaking havoc from the skies.

After the police arrived, Mercy was allowed into her apartment. When she saw the damage with her own two eyes, the vortex of rage consumed her once more.

The message painted on her wall made her want to scream.

"You first, asshole," she snarled.

Though her television and computer were still in the apartment, both screens had been smashed to smithereens. Her gun was gone.

As she and Kellan walked from room to room, inventorying the destruction, her blood pressure spiked and her head throbbed.

She wanted to cry when she saw all the beautiful antique tableware she'd spent months scouring E-bay for, now lying in a heap of broken shards and dust on the kitchen floor. In her bedroom, the brand-new damask bedding ensemble she'd purchased last week had been sliced to shreds. The pretty silver accent pillows were ripped open and flattened, while the white fiberfill littered her room like clumps of snow. Mercy quickly checked the drawer of her nightstand and bit back a scream. The bastard had even stolen all her vibes and sex toys.

Fear took a backseat to anger. Mercy was livid.

"Why? Why did he do this?" she spat. "Does he think I'll be so scared, so intimidated that I'll—what?—go running back to him and beg him to kill me?"

"No, angel. This is a warning."

She issued a humorless laugh. "Like his threats and pointing a gun to my head weren't enough?"

She didn't wait for him to answer. Mercy simply turned and stormed out of the bedroom, past the uniformed officers sprinkling graphite and dusting it away from nearly every available surface, and into the kitchen. Grabbing the broom and dustpan from the pantry, she began sweeping the remains of her dishes off the floor. Tears of anger stung her eyes and traveled down her cheeks.

Even before Kellan's strong hands gripped her shoulders, Mercy felt the heat of his body enveloping her from behind. She ached for his comfort but loathed it at the same time. She didn't want to feel weak or victimized. Kerr had stolen too much of her power, her control, and her peace of mind. She refused to crumble and give him even more.

Kellan leaned in close to her ear. "Stop, sweetheart. I'll make a phone call…we'll have this all cleaned up in a day or two. Come. Let's go sit down in the living room. Officer Amblin is here and needs to talk to you."

Mercy shoved the handle of the broom away, sending it crashing to the floor, then turned and jerked her chin up at him. "Fine. Let's go."

He stood like a statue, silently studying the contours of her face. Kellan stroked a finger down her cheek and along her jaw before leaning in close to her lips.

"I'm not the enemy. I know you're upset and if you need to, I'll turn you loose on the heavy bag in my gym, let you work the anger from your system. But until then, lose the attitude toward me."

Though his tone was deceivingly placid, his compelling command was bold and strong. For the first time since stepping into her apartment, Mercy felt as if she had a foundation under her feet. Kellan didn't expect or want her to deal with this infuriating carnage alone.

She briefly closed her eyes and nodded, then lifted on her toes and pressed her lips to his. "Thank you."

He simply winked and led her to the living room.

After answering a litany of questions and watching officers comb over her apartment like ants, she and Kellan were finally alone. Though she'd slept off and on most of the morning, it was past lunchtime and Mercy was exhausted.

"I'm taking you home and tucking you into bed," Kellan began. "I'll also be keeping the spare key to your apartment on my ring. Kerr doesn't need to redecorate a second time. Tell me what you'd like to take back to the house tonight, and I'll pack everything up for you."

With a knee-jerk reaction, Mercy opened her mouth to tell him she'd do it, but quickly snapped it shut.

"Good save, sweetheart." A knowing grin speared his lips.

"I *am* trying."

"You're doing fine."

His praise warmed her as they started toward the bedroom.

The storm had passed by the time they filled the trunk of Kellan's car with what few belongings she had left. Gray, dank clouds—matching Mercy's mood—scuttled overhead. As they made the short drive back to his house, she folded her hands in her lap and tried to relax. Just as she closed her eyes, her cell phone rang. When she pulled the device from her bag, Kellan held out his palm.

"No electronic devices. Remember?"

"But it's…" She snapped her mouth shut. Without even looking at the caller ID, she slapped the phone in his palm.

Kellan glanced at the screen. He placed the device facedown on his lap and continued driving while ignoring the incessant ring.

"Who is it?"

"Kerr."

Anger surged as she reached for the phone. As if anticipating her action, Kellan gripped her wrist and shook his head. "Let it go to voice mail, angel. If he leaves a message, it will likely be a threat. Those are admissible as evidence in a court of law."

Like a firefighter, Kellan's words extinguished the flames of anger inside her.

"Thank you, Your Honor. I didn't think of that. With the mess and the cops and chaos, I haven't had time to check my messages. If we're lucky, he's left a slew of them."

"One would do the job, but if there are more, that's all the better."

After arriving back at Kellan's house, he hauled her things up to the guest room, then they sat together on the couch and listened to the thirty-seven messages on her cell phone. All were from Kerr, except for the one call from her mom. As expected, the tone of the madman's threats grew exponentially gruesome and violent. Finally, Kellan turned the phone off and set it on the coffee table.

"I want you to rest. You've had a rough day. I'll phone something in for dinner and wake you when it arrives."

The fact that Kellan was instructing rather than asking didn't escape her attention, nor did the submissive thrills that shot through her.

"I'd like that. Thank you, Sir."

She desperately wanted to ask if he'd had a change of heart. If this was the beginning of the Dominance she'd hoped and prayed he'd bestow on her. But Mercy was afraid of jinxing the future…of him deciding instead to scoop up the breadcrumbs she'd been starving to sample.

She eased back on the couch and stretched out. The look of pride etched on his face when he draped the blanket over her was answer enough, for now.

"If you wake before dinner, I'll be in my office. I need to make some phone calls."

When he caressed his fingers over her cheek, Mercy captured his hand and placed a soft kiss in the center of his palm. "Thank you, for everything."

She watched his chest expand as he inhaled a deep breath. His blue eyes flickered with something deep and potent. Like a butterfly emerging from its cocoon, a flutter of hope unfurled inside her, and on fragile wings, it took flight.

"You don't need to thank me for wanting to keep you safe, angel. Now, sleep."

The house was silent but for Kellan's deep, rich voice resonating in the distance. Knowing he was near filled her with not only a sense of security but also contentment. She closed her eyes intending to simply rest but drifted off to sleep. Thankfully this time, Kerr didn't visit her dreams.

She woke to find Kellan sitting in a maroon wingback chair, reading a leather-bound book. When she sat up, he set the book in his lap and sent her a tender smile. Her pulse quickened. Mercy inwardly chided herself for being so ridiculously enchanted by the man.

"Did you sleep well?"

"Yes. Like a rock."

"I know." His smile turned into a wicked grin. "You were snoring so loudly, I came in to see if the furniture was moving."

"Ha ha." Mercy rolled her eyes. "I don't snore."

"How do you know?"

Just as the playful banter started getting fun, the doorbell rang. She shot him an anxious look.

"Relax. It's our dinner."

"How did they get through the gate?"

"I opened it from the security panel in the kitchen a few minutes ago. I'll get the door. Grab a bottle of white wine from the cooler in the kitchen. I'll meet you there in a minute." He stood and headed toward the foyer.

Mercy grinned at his retreating form. Oh, he loved giving out orders, but she loved following them even more. She hurried to the kitchen, opened the glass door of the cooler, and selected a bottle of

Cape Mentelle Sauvignon Blanc.

Kellan entered the kitchen and she raised a quizzical brow. "Is this one all right?"

"Perfect. Glasses are in the cabinet to your right and the opener's in the top drawer on your left."

Mercy opened the wine while he set dinner out on the table. The scent of seared beef, garlic, and other mouth-watering scents filled the room. Her stomach was gurgling as she removed the cork from the bottle. Moving in behind him, she placed the glasses at their plates and the wine in the center of the table.

He turned and gazed into her eyes. "Pour for me, little one."

As she filled his glass, Kellan sat down. His dissecting stare—the same one he always wore at the club—warmed her to the bone. She placed his glass beside his plate and slid into the chair across from him, anxious to lift the molded aluminum cover crimped over her food.

"Do you know how to perform a proper serve, angel?"

Proper serve?

"No, Sir. I didn't know there was such a thing, but I'd appreciate it if you'd tell me."

"Why don't I walk you through it?"

She could barely contain her elation. He was doing it…training her.

"I'd like that…like it very much."

When she was on her knees beside his chair, head lowered and thighs spread, thrusting the glass up to him with both hands, Mercy didn't like it…she fucking loved the peace enveloping her.

"Beautiful," Kellan whispered, lifting the glass from her fingers. "Simply stunning."

Mercy didn't want to move. She wanted to stay right there at his feet, wrapped in the glow of contentment and basking in the bliss of his approval.

She felt his fingers beneath her chin and raised her head. Kellan pressed the rim of the glass to her lips. "Take a sip."

As his Dominant gaze seared her flesh, the cold liquid flowed over her tongue. Her taste buds awakened beneath the fruity-tart flavor while her soul awakened to a new sense of submission. If Mercy possessed the power to stop time, this would be the one moment she'd want to be frozen in, forever.

"You'll be serving me a lot from now on, angel."

"I can't wait." She softly smiled.

"You may rise and enjoy your meal now."

Enjoy her meal? Butterflies were having a free-for-all in her stomach. Mercy wasn't sure she could even choke down a bite. Easing into her chair, she lifted the foil to find a slab of grilled steak, loaded baked potato, and steamed broccoli. Suddenly, she was famished.

"I know how much you love steak." Kellan smirked.

"How do you know that?"

"You told me on the way home from the hospital."

She didn't remember anything until he'd helped her out of his car in the garage.

"Why do I have a feeling that I said a lot of things I shouldn't have?"

"Tomorrow night, I'll order calzone for dinner," he said with a laugh.

"You're an evil, evil man," she giggled.

He shot her a wickedly sensual smile. "Like you can't imagine."

Oh, she could imagine…imagine him doing all kinds of dirty things to her. Mercy only hoped that one day he'd decide to make all her naughty fantasies come true.

KELLAN WOKE EARLY the next morning and peeked in on Mercy. She was still sleeping, so he padded to the kitchen to make coffee. He'd hoped that focusing on the mundane task might lessen the perpetual hard-on, determined to split the seam of his sweat pants.

It didn't.

If anything, knowing the intriguing sub would be beside him twenty-four seven for the next six days made him hornier than a sixteen-year-old.

He stood in the family room sipping coffee and looked out over the lake as another dreary, cloudy day dawned. Kellan had gone to sleep with the vision of Mercy on her knees during his impromptu lesson at dinner and had awakened with the same stunning sight filling his brain. While he wanted to dismiss it as nothing more than a passing whim, he couldn't. The staunch desire to guide her further pressed in all around him.

Mentoring her would take a heavy toll on his self-restraint and probably drive him to insanity, but watching her submissive beauty unfold had filled the dark and empty places inside him. The life she breathed into him was addicting.

"Son of a bitch," he muttered in resignation. "I *have* to train her."

Kellan's mind began to whirl with topics he intended to discuss with her. Things like safe words, limits, Dom and sub responsibilities, the sanctity of a collar, and a litany of fetishes. He was curious if the bold submissive had a few übër-kinky triggers. God, he hoped so.

After last night, he needed to keep her off her knees as much as possible or risk annihilating what little resolve he had left. Of course, the hungry Dominant beast within ached for her to be at his feet as he taught her how to kneel in both formal and informal settings, how to kneel up, how to center herself before a session, and the proper time to lift her head and address a Dom.

Not a Dom...*him*!

But most of all, Kellan wanted to teach her how to find serenity, confidence, and peace inside her submissive skin.

Some of her lessons were going to be downright torture.

Maybe you're a closet masochist, his subconscious taunted.

Kellan scoffed and shook his head.

"Good morning."

Mercy's husky sleepy voice seeped through his pores and sent a jolt to his system more potent than an entire pot of coffee. Kellan turned and smiled. Her eyelids were still heavy and her hair tousled. He knew then what she'd look like after a long night of unbridled sex.

Enticing.

Erotic.

All over again, fuckable.

Mercy dragged her fingers through her hair, attempting to tame the disheveled mass. "I know I look a sight, but I needed coffee before a shower."

"You look beautiful, as always."

A smile kicked up one corner of her mouth. "I bet you say that to all the girls."

"No. Just you, and Hannah, of course."

And Leena.

"Uh-huh," Mercy dubiously answered before disappearing into the kitchen.

Kellan knew he had to tell her about his wife, but not today. They had too much to do. He'd called Mika last night while Mercy was resting. The two men contacted a few others from Genesis. The plan was for everyone to meet up at her apartment in a few hours and clean up the destruction Kerr had left behind.

After they'd showered and dressed, Mercy whipped up a quick breakfast before heading to her place. She seemed hesitant to enter her apartment.

"You don't have to come in if you're not ready yet."

"No. I'm fine. It's just…I'm getting pissed again."

"I have a toy bag in my trunk. Do I need to go out and get a ball gag?" he teased.

She arched her brows at him. "I'll behave."

Surprisingly she did, at least until later in the afternoon, when the pizza arrived and Mercy reached in the freezer to retrieve ice for everyone's soda.

"Oh, my god," she growled.

"What?" He hurried to her side.

A rush of rage pelted his system as he stared at a photo of Mercy bent over a table with a cock shoved inside her ass.

"Don't look at…" Her words died out as she turned to see his eyes pinned to the picture. "I can't believe that bastard took pictures of…this."

"You didn't know he was photographing you?"

"No. Hell no!" Her lips were set in a flat, tight line as she began to tear the paper.

"Stop!" Kellan barked and lifted the photo from her hands. "That's evidence."

"There is no way I'm going to let a judge or jury see me like that. It's too embarrassing."

Kellan worked to tamp down the possessive jealousy coursing through his veins.

"I don't want this photo passed around a courtroom anymore than you do. But I'd hang on to it just in case…"

"In case of what?" she countered in a terse whisper. Mercy darted a quick glance toward the entrance to the kitchen. Either Mika, Drake,

Max, Joshua, Dylan, Nick, Ian, James and their subs hadn't heard Mercy's gasp at the discovery of the photo or they remained out of sight, granting them privacy. "There are plenty of witnesses from the club who saw Kerr point the damn gun to my head."

"Yes, but unless Amblin's team was able to lift any of Kerr's fingerprints yesterday, we don't have proof that *he* was the one responsible for the vandalism."

The mighty exhale that gushed from Mercy's lips expelled the bulk of indignation from her system as well. She moaned in defeat and dropped her forehead to Kellan's chest.

"I just wish this whole mess was over instead of beginning."

He wrapped his arms around her and held her tight. "I do, too, angel."

It was sometime after lunch that Mercy emerged from her embarrassed funk. Of course, Savannah, Julianna, Trevor, Samantha, Mellie, and Liz were the obvious reason. It somehow helped when Trevor shared his feelings on the abuse he'd endured, and Mellie's experiences with Kerr. At least Mercy knew she wasn't the only victim of an unjust world.

When they were finished removing all traces of Kerr from her apartment, Julianna rubbed her barely visible baby bump and promised to bring her computer by the house in a few days and help order new bedding and dishes.

"No electronics," Kellan reminded with a stern expression.

"I'll get an idea of what she's looking for and limit the time she can look at any images to five seconds." Julianna grinned. "Will that be acceptable, Sir?"

"Welcome to my world," Mika mumbled to Kellan with a crooked grin.

"Subs. I swear!" Kellan rolled his eyes. "Yes, girl. That is permissible, but not a second over five, understood?"

Julianna drew an X over her heart with her finger. "Absolutely, Sir."

"I want to come over and cyber shop, too," Trevor pouted.

"Why don't all of you come over? I'll grill some burgers if it's not raining," Kellan suggested.

"I think he just wants to keep an eye on you, sis," Trevor whispered then started to giggle. "Hide all the clocks and watches you can find tonight after he goes to bed."

"Boy!" Drake thundered in warning. "If you don't stop trying to cause trouble, I'll bring a world of hurt down on you."

Trevor purred softly. "Promise?"

"Like you won't be able to stand, boy. Don't push me, you sassy slut. Or I'll be the only one reading Hope a story before bed."

Trevor paled at Drake's threat to ban him from tucking in their infant daughter.

"Forget I said anything," he whispered to Mercy loud enough for everyone to hear.

Though she laughed along with the others, Kellan could see confusion swimming in her eyes.

After many thanks when the work was finished, and a round of good-byes, Kellan and Mercy drove toward his house. He held her hand as the skies above them grew darker.

"What was bothering you earlier…when Drake and Trevor were bantering?"

"It surprised me that Trevor was so…mouthy," she replied.

"That's Trevor. He never holds back what he's thinking, at least not since I've known him."

"But isn't he disrespecting Drake by doing that?"

"No. Well, I mean, to some it might appear that way. In the simplest terms, it's a cry for Drake to reinforce his command. Trevor's been through a hell none of us can truly understand. They've both been through the wringer. Not only that, but having a baby in the house demands a lot of attention. I think Trevor simply wants the reassurance that he's firmly and irrevocably under Drake's thumb."

"That makes sense, but isn't that a form of Topping from the bottom?"

Kellan shrugged. "Evidently Drake doesn't perceive it that way, or I suspect he'd staple Trevor's mouth shut."

Mercy sucked in a hiss and cringed.

"What I'm trying to say is that every relationship is different. What works for one couple or polyamorous relationship isn't guaranteed to work for another. That's why communication is necessary. It establishes the parameters that make a Dom/sub relationship fulfilling."

Mercy nodded as she sat absorbing his words.

"Don't worry. I'll do my best to help you gain a better understanding."

She turned and pinned him with a look of anticipation. "So, are you saying that you've decided to train me?"

Kellan pondered her question for several long seconds. "Yes, I suppose I am."

Mercy's chin quivered slightly as a wobbly smile spread over her lips. "Thank you, Sir. I won't let you down."

He sent her a gentle smile. "I know you won't, gorgeous."

Though she'd be a constant and brutal test of his willpower, Kellan needed Mercy to cast away the shadows within him and draw him out to the light as much as she needed him to do the same.

Another wedge of anxiety melted from his shoulders.

OVER THE NEXT three days, Mercy eagerly approached each lifestyle discussion with an open mind and more questions than Kellan imagined possible. She drank in every nuance of Dominance and submission like a sponge. While Mercy's headaches had vanished, he still watched for any signs of a relapse.

Every night at dinner, she would slide to her knees in the kitchen and raise a beverage to him with such grace and beauty it shook him to his Dominant core. He wanted to cinch a fist in her hair, drag her up and lay her out over the table, then drive his cock balls deep inside her precious yielding body. Sheer will kept him from it…for now.

Kerr had still evaded capture. The Chicago PD hadn't been able to locate the prick, and Kellan was growing worried and frustrated. He didn't let Mercy out of his sight. Not even when Julianna came to visit with her laptop and several other subs and sat out on the deck in the unseasonably warm weather, oohing and ahhing over items to replace the ones Kerr had destroyed.

When he heard Mercy lament about buying a new computer to her friends, an idea formed in Kellan's mind. While she and the others were in the kitchen whipping up lunch, he'd snuck upstairs and wrapped her broken laptop in a small tote bag along with a note to Mika.

Hours later, when the subs began to leave, Kellan gave the bag to Julianna and asked her to return it to Mika. She gave him a strange look but thankfully didn't ask any questions.

Kellan had thought buying Mercy a new computer and transferring her old files to the new one would be a wonderful surprise. Unfortunately, he'd inadvertently opened Pandora's box. After seeing the new device, Mercy began relentlessly begging to spend an hour or two "playing" with the new computer. When she refused to stop, Kellan was forced to hand down her first punishment.

After binding her wrists and ankles to the arms and legs of a kitchen chair, he placed her cell phone and computer on the table in front of her. The MP3 player he *found* tucked in the bedside drawer of the guest room remained in his pants pocket.

"You will focus on the items in front of you, angel. You are not to lift your eyes and look at me, or your punishment will begin all over again. You will answer only when I ask you a question. Is that clear?"

"Yes, Sir."

"Do you have any questions regarding what I have outlined?"

"No, Sir."

In pure interrogation style, he placed his hands behind his back and slowly walked back and forth. He watched her intently, making sure her stare didn't stray from the devices he'd placed on the table.

"Why are you banned from using these?"

"Because I had a concussion."

"You have," he corrected.

"But I—"

"That wasn't a question," he interrupted with a low but clipped tone. Kellan couldn't help but smile as a tremor of blatant excitement rippled through her. "You'll keep your explanations to yourself unless I ask for them. Is that clear?"

"Yes, Sir."

"To make sure that you followed Dr. Brooks' instructions, I rearranged my court cases to keep you here with me. Why do you suppose I did that?"

"Because you were worried about me, Sir?"

"Yes, indeed I was, but there's another reason. Do you know what that might be?"

"No, Sir."

"Because I know you, little one. I knew you wouldn't last seven days without picking up your phone or logging in to your computer…or perhaps sneaking a listen to some music?"

When he pulled the music player out of his pocket and placed it beside her phone, Mercy closed her eyes and wrinkled her face. She was definitely having an *oh, shit* moment.

"Yes, my devious little minx…you've been busted…busted big-time." He moved in and stepped behind her. Gently brushing her hair to one side, Kellan leaned in close to her ear as she shivered. "What do you think I should do about this, hmm?"

Long, silent seconds passed as she seemingly weighed his words. "Is that a rhetorical question, or are you genuinely asking for my input, Sir?"

He couldn't help but grin, but Kellan wasn't about to lose the upper hand. He dragged his tongue up the side of her neck, drinking in her silky moan as she tilted her head to the side granting him more access. Unable to resist he sank his teeth into the plump flesh of her earlobe and tugged lightly. Mercy sucked in a quivering gasp and gripped the arms of the chair.

He would never grow tired of the erotic way she responded to him. Without a word, he released the silk ropes binding her ankles and wrists and extended his hand.

Mercy stared at his open palm before lifting her soulful, yearning eyes to meet his.

"Do you trust me, angel?"

"With my life, Sir," she answered.

She slid her fingers into his waiting hand. An urgent need to crush her to his chest and never let go uncoiled inside him. The looming anxiety that Mercy would soon return to her apartment and her life crept down his spine. He didn't want her to leave. Didn't want to be forced into the dark, empty exile again.

As he drew her into his arms, Kellan closed his eyes and savored the feel of her soft body pressed so perfectly to his. He was powerless to alter his past or predict his future. All he could do was imprint each life-altering moment he spent with this captivating and sensual sub deep in his soul. Kellan had no doubt each memory would warm his empty nights for years to come.

He buried his face in her soft hair and inhaled deeply as he forced the depressing thoughts from his mind. "Your safe word is now diamond."

"Diamond?" Mercy repeated curiously.

"Yes. You constantly blind me with your bright and shimmering light, angel."

She pulled back and studied his face. A wealth of happiness glistened in her eyes. "That's the sweetest thing any man has ever said to me."

"Get used to it." He sent her a crooked smile.

A pensive expression fell over her face. "Are you going to force me to use my safeword, Sir?"

"I don't plan to. I simply aim to instill the importance of taking care of yourself…doing what you've been instructed to do. Dr. Brooks wouldn't be pleased to discover you've ignored his orders any more than I am. Remember our discussion about submissive responsibilities?"

"Yes, Sir."

"Then I shouldn't have to remind you to eat, sleep, and care for your physical and mental health in order to represent your Dominant in the best light possible."

"Is that a roundabout way of saying that you've assumed the role of my…my Dom now, Sir?"

Hope was written all over her face. It knocked the wind out of him like a punch to the gut. His heart wanted to say yes. But his conscience wouldn't allow it.

Kellan sent her grim and melancholy smile. "No, angel. I'm not. I'm simply your mentor."

Mercy lowered her lids and nodded. "I'm ready, Sir."

"For?"

"My punishment," she answered bravely.

"Very well. Follow me."

Kellan led her through the alcove separating the dining room and kitchen. He opened the door to the basement and descended the stairs, hyperaware of Mercy trailing close behind. Striding past his home gym, he drew open the door to a small dungeon. After Leena's accident, he'd poured his fear and frustration into creating the play space. Foolishly convincing himself that his wife would fully recover, he'd planned to surprise her when she returned home. But his wife was floating between heaven and earth, never to return.

Bringing Mercy to the dungeon he'd designed for Leena sent a tinge of guilt to stain his conscience. But the past five days he'd spent with Mercy, she'd taught him that lumbering aimlessly through life wasn't living, but merely existing. He found it ironic that the teacher had inadvertently become the student.

Mercy stood in the middle of the room, taking in the sight of the St. Andrews Cross, bondage table, and spanking bench he'd painstakingly sawed, sanded, and stained.

A palpable wave of apprehension rolled off her as she dropped her chin and gazed at the floor. Kellan greedily absorbed her angst and blended it with his power. He aimed to stress the importance of obeying directions as he set her submissive soul free.

"Strip," he commanded.

CHAPTER EIGHT

Mercy jerked her head up and shot him a deer-in-the-headlights stare. She wasn't embarrassed about taking off her clothes. She'd stripped dozens of times for Kerr. It was the fact that Kellan had commanded her to take off her clothes that blew Mercy's socks off.

"Eyes on the floor, angel." His low, firm tone had her girl parts melting like spun sugar.

After spending the past five days with Kellan in almost constant arousal, Mercy feared that his slightest touch would make her shatter beneath a massive O.

"We've discussed protocol. Have you already forgotten what you've learned?"

She shook her head and lowered her gaze.

Mercy had strived to keep from disappointing Kerr for fear of his punishments.

The idea of failing Kellan and letting him down physically hurt her heart.

He'd tapped into a whole other level of submission she'd never felt before…unlocked some primitive and elemental need to surrender. An arousing hunger began rising inside her.

"When I am in command of you, whether in this dungeon or the one at the club, I expect you to use your words when you answer me. Is that clear?"

Kellan had moved in close behind her. She could feel his breath caress her shoulders.

"Yes, Sir."

"Good. When I give you an instruction, I don't ever want to be forced to repeat myself, angel."

Holy hell!

Mercy had watched Kellan work other subs at the club before, but she'd never been on the receiving end. His Dominance was enthralling…dizzying…captivating. She didn't waste another second; Mercy peeled off her clothes.

"I'll use my words from now on, Sir."

"Yes. Like a sinful bar of candy, I aim to unwrap all the sweet submission inside you, let it melt over your tongue, and let you feast on serenity."

She'd much rather he unzip his fly and let her feast on his cock until it melted all over her tongue, but kept that fantasy to herself.

"Kneel before the cross, girl. Clear your head and ready yourself for a session like we talked about yesterday."

"Yes, Sir."

Lowering to her knees on the thick, plush carpet, Mercy bowed her head and closed her eyes. When she'd entered the small but tastefully decorated dungeon, she'd noticed the floggers, paddles, whips, and crops hanging from individual hooks along the walls. The tools of bliss and torture were displayed the same way at Club Genesis. She wondered what implements he would choose for her punishment. Would Kellan stop if she used her safe word? Mercy didn't have a lot of faith in safe words. They hadn't done much to protect her ass so far.

He's not Kerr. This is Kellan. He isn't punishing you for his pleasure. You fucked up. Remember?

Oh, yes. Mercy remembered the disappointment that sluiced in her veins when he placed her MP3 player on the table.

"Is there a reason you're not trying to clear you mind? I can hear you thinking from here."

She started to lift her head at the sound of his voice across the room but stopped herself in the nick of time.

Dammit. She wanted to clear her head but couldn't shut off her brain. Hearing his words, Mercy was doubly distracted now. She was curious to see what toys he'd selected, making it even harder to remain in her submissive pose.

"I'm trying, Sir, but it's hard."

"Then ask for my help." Kellan knelt down in front of her and gently raised her chin with his fingers. Pride and reassurance glistened in his compassionate stare. "Why are we here?"

"So you can punish me."

"No. We're here so you can make amends for disobeying the rules. Tell me, how do you feel inside knowing that you've disappointed me?"

"It feels lousy."

"I'm glad to hear that."

"Why?"

"Because that tells me that you yearn to please. That submission isn't simply something fun and exciting to do, a role to play, but that you genuinely feel the need to make me happy."

"I do."

"Then why did you sneak the device into your room?"

Mercy swallowed tightly. God, she didn't want to confess the reason, but Kellan would sense a lie a mile away. Of that she was sure.

"I didn't pack it from my apartment with the intent to use it. I just tossed it into the duffel bag that day."

"Go on."

She exhaled heavily and cast her gaze back to the floor. "A couple nights ago, I couldn't sleep. So I thought maybe a little music might help me relax."

"Why were you tense?"

"I-I was thinking about you," she mumbled.

"Oh? What exactly were you thinking?"

Mercy could hear the smile in his voice. Yeah, he was going to love what she confessed next.

Shit!

"I wondered what it would be like if instead of telling me good night from the doorway, you…well, you crawled in bed with me."

"I see. Raise your head and look at me, girl. Tell me what you imagined me doing to you then."

Mercy swallowed tightly and gazed into his eyes once more. His supportive expression had been replaced with carnal fire.

"Everything," she whispered on a trembling breath.

"Every dirty little thing you could think of?" He asked with a knowing smirk.

She blanched. Something about the words he chose felt hauntingly familiar.

"I know you fantasize about me when you masturbate. You told me the night I brought you here from the hospital."

Mercy's eyes grew wide. Her stomach swirled. She felt her cheeks catch fire. Good god. Had she blabbed every detail to him that night? Embarrassment pulsed so vehemently through her she wanted to melt into the carpet.

"I'll share a secret with you, gorgeous. I fantasize about you while I'm fisting my cock. I dream about all the dirty little things I'd love to do to you as well."

The floodgates between her legs opened. A ripple of hunger made her clit and nipples tighten and throb. A tiny moan rolled off the back of her throat. She ached to wrap her arms around his neck and kiss him…slide her tongue past his full lips and feast on his mouth. Press her naked body against him and writhe all over him until Kellan ripped off his clothes and fucked her hard right there on the floor.

As if reading her mind, he slanted his mouth over hers and took possession of her with a savage kiss. He thrust his tongue deep as he gripped her shoulders in his strong, capable hands. Mercy moaned as she wrapped her tongue around his, gliding up and down as if it were his cock, and swallowed his feral growl.

Kellan cupped her breasts. Squeezing and massaging her aching orbs, he plucked and pinched her nipples until she pulled from his mouth, and tossed back her head crying out in bliss.

A low, sultry chuckle rumbled from Kellan's chest. He released her breasts, giving one last tug on her nipples, then stood. The bulging erection tenting his trousers, taunted her. Mercy wanted to reach out and release his steely length and suck him down her throat.

"You're not here for pleasure, my wicked little angel. You're here for punishment."

"Beat me. Bruise me. I don't care. Just please, Sir…fuck me when you're done…please?"

Kellan's nostrils flared. His cock lurched against his zipper. A look of indecision fluttered across his face before he clenched his jaw and slowly shook his head. "Who makes the rules, little one?"

"You do, Sir."

"Exactly. Rise and place yourself over the spanking bench. Keep your ass raised up high in the air for me, girl."

On shaky legs, she stood and complied. She shivered when she raised her ass and the cool air of the room met her wet and heated core. Kellan moved in close behind her. The air stirred and Mercy could smell the heady scent of her own feminine musk.

"Even prettier than I imagined," he murmured. "Your pussy is so pink and swollen and wet. You make my mouth water and my cock scream, girl."

"Oh, god," she groaned. "Please…oh, yes please."

"What exactly are you begging for?"

"Your mouth, your fingers, your cock…all of you, Sir. I *need* all of you."

Kellan hissed out a curse. "Is that why we're in the dungeon?"

Frustration spiked. A low, suffering moan slid from her throat. "No, Sir."

"No, and it's a pity, because there's nothing I'd love more than to drive my cock deep inside your glistening cunt. But you haven't earned that reward yet, have you?"

"No, Sir." Mercy planned to remedy that, and soon.

"Shall we begin and get this unpleasantness over?"

I'd rather begin with you fucking my brains out.

Mercy kept the smartassed comment to herself and nodded. "Yes Sir."

In preparation for the initial burst of pain, she squeezed her eyes closed, clenched her butt cheeks, and held her breath. When Kellan simply skimmed a palm over her ass, she jolted and exhaled. His reverent caress felt as if he were worshiping her flesh. But that was the duty of a submissive, not a Dom. The lines of command and surrender blurred. She had no idea now what to expect with this man. Mercy felt as if she'd been tossed into stormy seas.

"I *do* plan to warm you up first," he whispered with a hint of amusement. "No transgression deserves brutality."

His caveat was music to her ears. The tendrils of dread bled away.

The first stinging blow sent a chill racing up her spine, but the intimate contact of his hand to her flesh ignited a slow fire to coil beneath her clit. The punishment Kellan delivered was unlike any she'd experienced. The synapses in her brain didn't know how to process the delicious combination of pleasure and pain.

"Rules are put in place for a reason."

To emphasize his words, he landed another slap against her flesh.

"To keep you safe or, in this case, to help you heal."

Smack.

The biting sting spread out over her flesh in a luscious burn that engulfed her lower back and thighs. The sensation was as confusingly soothing as the indulgent tone of Kellan's voice.

Smack.

"The only pleasure I gain from punishing you is the feel of your succulent ass on my hand."

Smack.

"Of course, watching your sinful cheeks turn a pretty glowing red doesn't suck, either."

Smack.

"Your quivering gasps will continue to echo in my ears for a long time."

Smack.

Mercy whimpered and rolled her hips in an attempt to assuage the increasing ache between her legs.

Smack.

"You're so fucking gorgeous all splayed out before me with your red ass in the air, my sweet sub."

Kellan continued to praise her as he landed his palm against her searing flesh. No longer cognizant of her surroundings, she focused on his rich, deep voice sliding over her flesh and the rhythmic slap of his hand.

She felt as if she were floating.

Not outside her body but deep inside her mind.

Floating to some foreign place where her conscious and soul melded.

Enveloped in a shimmering white light of peace and beauty, Mercy sailed on in this strange silent serenity. There were no worries fluttering through her mind. No fears. Nothing but the reassurance of Kellan's wide hand as he guided her into a surreal world of buoyant beauty.

She'd never felt so free...so complete in all her life.

Mercy dipped and soared inside the captivating bliss.

Hours, minutes, or days later—she wasn't sure—she lifted her heavy eyelids. She was no longer on the spanking bench but cradled in a soft cotton blanket and nestled against Kellan's bare chest as he climbed the spiral staircase. She didn't know when or where he'd removed his shirt, and at that moment she didn't care. Mercy was far too captivated with his velvet-blue eyes locked on hers and the slow smile stretching his lips. Her heart sputtered, and the heat that engulfed her ass seemed to spread through her whole body.

"Welcome back, angel," he whispered. "Did you enjoy your flight?"

Mercy couldn't help but grin as she gave him a listless nod. She felt drunk, as if everything were moving in slow motion, especially her brain. She tried to gather the fragmented pieces of reality, but the peaceful nirvana within beckoned her to sail on a little longer. She closed her eyes once more.

"Oh, yes, but I don't think I've landed yet," she answered on a dreamy sigh.

"I don't think you have, either. Sail on, angel. I've got you."

The only response she could muster was a satisfied purr.

Kellan laid her down on a soft surface and she felt him stretch out beside her. Mercy opened her eyes once more to find she was in the guest room and in bed. As her lids slid shut, she snuggled in close to his warm body, laid her head on his chest, and sighed. He stroked her head and combed his fingers through her hair.

The beat of his heart and the rumble of his voice as he suffused her with praise, echoed in her ears. Slowly, Mercy began rising from the dreamy depths, becoming more aware of Kellan and her surroundings. She raised her arm, stunned at how heavy her limb felt, and brushed a whip of Kellan's charcoal hair from his forehead before breaking the comfortable silence.

"Thank you for…I don't know how to describe it. I've never felt anything like this before."

"Endorphins. You've been riding them for quite some time. Did you enjoy it?"

"Oh, yes. Enjoy doesn't come close to how incredible I feel."

Kellan chuckled. "I think I might have created a brat."

"What do you mean?"

"I mean…you enjoyed your punishment too much. I'll have to come up with a suitable alternative next time."

"If you keep sending me off to heaven like you just did, you'll never have to punish me again. I'll be the best submissive on the planet."

"Uh-huh," he grunted with a hint of disbelief.

"I will," she protested. "You'll see."

Mercy placed her palm on his chest before skimming it up and down his flesh. Gliding her hand lower, she dragged her fingers over his engorged cock. She felt his muscles tense as he grabbed her wrist and lifted her hand away.

"Did I give you permission to touch me?"

"No, Sir. It's just that I-I want to make you feel good."

He slid his fingers into her mane, gathering the strands into his fist. Pulses of pain and pleasure spread over her scalp as he tugged her head back and gazed down at her.

"Don't you know by now? I always feel good when I'm with you."

He bent and claimed her lips in a hungry, possessive kiss.

KELLAN ATE HER silky mouth as the image of her luscious wet pussy burned in his brain. A lesser man would have caved and fucked her raw over the spanking bench. He still wasn't quite sure how he'd unearthed the willpower to resist. Lying beside her warm, naked body was taking an even bigger toll on him. His dick had been hard for hours, but teaching her this lesson was necessary. So was providing her with plenty of aftercare. Easing a sub back to earth after a session was as vital as soaring her into subspace. But damn. He needed to come…needed to relieve the pressure stretching the skin of his cock to the point of pain.

Mercy eased from his lips. Peppering his jaw with soft kisses, she slowly inched her tongue down his neck. She slid her hands over his chest, leaving a trail of heat that felt so fucking good Kellan could only close his eyes and bask in her attention. She kissed her way over his collarbones and down to his nipples. Mercy traced her sinful tongue around each circle of brown flesh and kissed each taut peak. He growled and squeezed the fist in her hair tightly, feeling her tug against his grip to drag her mouth lower still.

When she began to unbutton his trousers, Kellan knew he needed to seize control, but the feel of her wicked mouth roaming his flesh felt too damn good. He hadn't felt the rush of pleasure consume him in this way for too damn long. Mercy carefully eased his zipper down and Kellan groaned when his cock sprang free.

"Oh, god."

The tone of awe in her whisper yanked him from his carnal trance. A wave of panic crashed through him. Kellan sat up and snatched her hand away as she reached for his shaft. Mercy sent him a pleading stare.

"Please don't make me stop," she begged.

The minute she licked her lips, he was a goner. Kellan couldn't refuse her plea to worship his cock anymore than he could fly. But he refused to lie back and let her take control over him.

"Move to the side of the bed and get on your knees." His voice was husky and laced with need.

Her eyes widened with excitement. Mercy scampered off the bed and onto her knees.

With his gaze locked on her, Kellan stood, removed his trousers, and then sat down on the side of the bed. She was the vision of his dreams…pure unadulterated sin.

Her plump lips, level with his cock, were parted invitingly.

Need and hunger glistened in her eyes.

The scent of her pussy clung to every breath he inhaled.

Demand rolled through him, and it took everything Kellan had not to grip her hair and slam his impatient dick straight down her throat. He tempered his fervent lust and dragged a finger down her cheek.

"Take me inside your pretty mouth. Worship my cock."

Dropping her jaw open, she leaned in. Her moist breath caressed his dripping crest.

Kellan bit back a savage roar.

When she wrapped her plump lips around him, he felt as if he'd died and gone to heaven. His nerve endings were on fire and he was going up in flames. The gentle suction of her mouth and glide of her velvet tongue had him nearly losing his load.

Each drag of her lips, flick of her tongue, and scrape of her teeth over his throbbing veins sent him soaring to an even higher level of bliss. He struggled to harness the come churning in his balls. He didn't want to embarrass himself and end this too soon.

"Mercy," he choked out in a strangled whisper. "Your mouth feels like heaven."

As if emboldened by his praise, she cupped his sac, and massaged his heavy orbs in her palm. Kellan watched her lips slide up and down his glistening shaft as she enveloped him with wet, silky heat.

His head swam.

The room swayed.

He knew he wasn't going to last long, but fuck if he'd let go this soon. Clenching his jaw, he reached out and gripped her hair, then eased her off his shaft.

"You'll swallow every drop, little one. Understood?"

"Oh, yes, Sir. It would be an honor." Her voice was low and sultry. A shiver raced up his spine.

"More. Work that eager little tongue all around me."

She opened her mouth, prepared to engulf him again, but Kellan held her head firmly in place. Unable to fulfill her quest, Mercy whimpered and shot him a pleading stare. He simply shook his head. A little pout settled over her mouth before she smiled and extended her tongue, bathing the tip of his throbbing crest with soft, beguiling flicks.

She was going to be the death of him. At that particular moment, Kellan couldn't think of a better way to go than with his cock deep down her throat. Provoked by the thought, he tugged her to his shaft. His eyes rolled to the back of his head as she swallowed him all the way to the base of his stalk. Though he could barely breathe, Kellan guided her by her head, setting a safe tempo at which he could both revel in the feel of her wicked mouth but also keep from exploding all over her tongue.

Mercy rolled her hips from side to side. Kellan imagined her clit, swollen and peeking out from beneath the thin membrane, needy and aching for relief as well.

"Reach between your legs and rub your clit for me, angel. I want to watch you shatter as I fill your belly with my seed."

Her eyes grew wide. The glassy, unfocused sheen reflecting in them told Kellan that she was as desperate to shatter as he was.

"You don't have permission to come yet, sub. Is that clear?"

Her grunted reply sent a vibration to ripple over his dick. Kellan gritted his teeth and hissed.

As she bobbed up and down on his stalk and strummed her clit, he gazed at the glorious, beautiful woman before him. Her thick lashes lay against her delicate face, and her smooth cheeks concaved beneath the mind-bending suction she bestowed. Kellan lost a little more of his heart with each wonderfully wicked lash of her tongue. Mercy wasn't merely worshiping his cock; she was making love to him…pouring out her entire soul for him to claim and protect.

Her tiny whimpers and mewls zapped his system like bolts of lightning.

The thunder of release rolled through him. He gripped her head and shuttled in and out of her mouth in sharp, rapid strokes. His balls drew up and his vision blurred.

"Come hard for me, angel. Come, now!"

She clamped her mouth around him and sucked with all her might. He felt her muscles tense before her muffled scream tore over his blistering length.

Mercy's body quivered as the orgasm consumed her.

Kellan roared as their storms of ecstasy collided.

White-hot lightning engulfed his tightening balls, and Kellan gave up trying to hold back a second longer. His cock expanded and thick ropes of come jettisoned from the head, showering her tongue and throat. Mercy gulped greedily as she swallowed his seed. Reaching up, she wrapped her slender hand around his shaft and milked him dry while she licked and lapped him clean.

Both of them trembled in aftershocks as she released his shaft. Kellan slid a finger beneath her chin and sent her a sated smile.

"That was incredible."

Her cheeks grew pink and a coy smile tugged her lips. "It was, Sir. Thank you."

Kellan lifted her off the floor and pulled her to his chest as he slumped back onto the bed. She fell limp across his chest and issued a contented sigh. He closed his eyes and drank in the feel of her soft, naked flesh meshed against him.

Long minutes later, their silent bliss was interrupted by the ring of his cell phone. The unique ringtone cut through his carnal fog like an ax. It was the nursing home. In one fluid movement, he rolled Mercy to his side and lurched out of bed. Fumbling with the pocket of his trousers, Kellan finally pulled the device free.

"Hello?" he answered hastily.

"Mr. Graham?"

"Yes."

"It's Lucia. You need to come quickly. I'm sorry"—her voice cracked—"but Leena suffered a stroke a few minutes ago."

Kellan's gut coiled. His throat closed up and he felt like he couldn't breathe.

A stroke? God no. This couldn't be happening. Not yet.

He wasn't ready to lose her.

Hannah.

He needed to call Hannah.

"Is she…"

"She's still alive. But we don't know for how much longer. I'm so sorry. Would you like me to call your daughter for you?"

"No. I'll do it. I'm on my way."

Kellan grabbed his pants off the floor and frantically looked around the room for his shirt, but couldn't find it. He raced out to the hall and sprinted to his bedroom. He ripped a cotton polo from its hanger and yanked it over his head as he slid on a pair of loafers. Patting his pockets, he felt his keys and turned toward the hall.

Mercy stood in the doorway wearing a look of confusion. "I take it you're leaving?"

Guilt inundated him in a deluge of shame. While another woman had been sucking his cock, his wife had lain alone in an empty room having a stroke.

"Yes. Wait here. I'll be back…I-I'm not sure when. But I'll be back."

"Is something wrong?"

Dammit! There wasn't time to waste explaining everything to Mercy. He scrubbed a hand through his hair and pinned her with a sorrowful gaze.

"Kellan, you're scaring me. Is it Hannah? Is she sick? Has she been in an accident?"

"No! It's my wife," he blurted as he rushed past her, raced down the stairs, and sprinted into the garage.

MERCY STOOD IN the middle of the hallway, mouth open, body shaking, and mind racing. She felt as if she'd just been punched in the gut and slapped in the face.

Wife?

Wife!

WIFE!

"What do you mean your *wife*, you son of a bitch?" she screamed.

There was no answer to her cry as it echoed through the empty house. Kellan was already gone…gone back to his fucking wife!

He wasn't divorced at all. The cheating man-whore had been married the whole damn time.

And just where the hell had the little missus been? she wondered.

Had his wife been out of town on business?

"When the cat's away, the mice will play."

And oh, how Kellan had played…played Mercy to the nth degree. Not only had the prick conveniently moved her into his palatial estate, he'd pretended he wasn't interested in teaching her submission. No doubt that had been part of the big plan to make her feel as if he was doing her some big-assed fucking favor when he finally relented. Make her feel as if she *owed* him something for his sacrifice. Kellan wasn't a stupid man. He had to know that once Mercy found out he was married, she'd walk the fuck out and not give him a second glance at the club.

"You got some balls, mister…big fucking sick and twisted balls."

She had no facts, only assumptions that zipped through her head so furiously she couldn't make sense of the clusterfuck.

Did he and his wife have an open marriage?

That would certainly explain why Hannah wasn't judging the judge's actions. She probably wouldn't fault her own mother for spending the last week banging the Chicago Bears football team, either.

Talk about dysfunctional.

"It doesn't matter," Mercy spat out loud.

Whatever *understanding* Kellan and his wife had regarding their vows, or rather, the breach of them, didn't change the fact that he was married.

If he'd respected Mercy at all, he *would* have fucking told her.

Maybe they're separated.

"Shut up," she barked at her subconscious. "I will not start grasping at straws or making excuses for the misogynistic prick. I did enough of that with Kerr."

There's only one way to find out.

Yearning to silence the pesky voice in the back of her head, Mercy stormed into Kellan's room. She hadn't stepped foot inside his private domain since she'd arrived. She wished now that she would have started snooping around from the very start.

With long, determined strides, she entered his closet. Mercy had expected to see half of the massive room chock full of designer women's wear. But she didn't. The closet contained Kellan's dark suits, dress shirts, and an assortment of shoes.

Nothing was adding up.

There wasn't a shred of evidence to prove he was married. But he *had* to be. No man on the planet referred to his ex as his *wife*. Well not many. Most referred to their exes as the alimony queen, Satan's succubus, and a whole host of other derogatory terms. *Wife* was far too affectionate for the most amicable divorce.

Fuming, Mercy turned and started to leave his room. As she passed the dresser, she stopped dead in her tracks and stared at a photo of a younger, heart-stoppingly handsome image of Kellan dressed in a dark gray tux. Snuggled up beside him was a stunning blonde—who bore an uncanny resemblance to Hannah—wearing a white lace wedding dress. Their smiles were blinding…glowing with happiness and a love so profound it ripped Mercy's heart in two.

Tears burned her eyes.

"You asshole!" she cried. "Why did you do this to me? Didn't we…didn't *I* mean anything to you? We shared something special. I felt it! Is this all a game to you? Or was it some twisted, heartless kind of joke? Well, guess what, cocksucker? I'm *not* fucking laughing!"

Angrily swiping her tears, Mercy ran to the guest room. The wrinkled comforter on the bed mocked her and the intimacy she'd shared with Kellan. Howling with rage, she picked up the lamp from the dresser and heaved it across the room. The ceramic base exploded into a million pieces while the shade bounced and landed on its side, bent and battered.

"You fucking prick! I can't believe you played me. I should have learned my lesson after Kerr. All men are gutless pigs!" Succumbing to the anguish clawing inside her, Mercy crumpled to the floor and sobbed.

Long minutes passed as she tried to pull herself together and will away the pulsing undertow of pain. She vacillated between rage and regret as she nursed her wounded pride.

Kellan would be home sometime…but Mercy had no intention of being here to greet him. She'd formulated an escape plan as she sat sobbing like a child.

Get your ass off the pity pot.
Pack your shit.
Leave.

Drying her eyes on the sleeve of her shirt, Mercy dragged herself off the floor and began packing. When she'd finished collecting her things, she hauled the duffel bag and box to the foyer. As she made her way into the kitchen, a lump clogged her throat as she gazed at her electronics spread out over the table and the strands of silky rope Kellan had used to bind her, still lying on the floor.

"I refuse to cry another fucking tear for that man!" she bit out angrily, willing the tears back that filled her eyes.

Mercy palmed her phone and shoved it into the pocket of her jeans. She grabbed her computer and MP3 player, then stomped to the foyer and placed them with the rest of her things before tapping the Uber app on her phone. When she stepped outside, the icy wind stole her breath. Mercy darted back into the house and swiped a winter coat from the closet. She'd mail the damn thing back to Kellan next week. After hauling the box and duffel outside, Mercy groaned when she saw that the security gate was closed.

"Best-laid plans and all that shit," she hissed as she placed her belongs against the fence.

A few minutes later, a dark blue SUV pulled into the driveway. Mercy waved her arm through the bars, motioning for the driver. A big, burly man with colorful tattoos adorning his thick arms strolled toward her.

"Am I part of a prison break or something?" he asked with a chuckle.

"Something like that, yeah." Mercy turned on the charm. "My boyfriend went out for a while, probably to go bang some nasty skank. We haven't been getting along so well. He changed the damn code on the gate, and now I'm stuck. Do you think…if I lifted my stuff over the fence, you could maybe…um…"

"It's been a couple weeks since I helped a damsel in distress. Let's do this."

After hefting her things over the gate, she climbed the brick face and jumped into the prickly shrubs lining the outside perimeter.

In a matter of minutes, she was heading home.

Home.

Her once safe haven had been ransacked and vandalized. Mercy wondered if she'd ever let her guard down inside her apartment again. She didn't know how or why, but in a few short days, Kellan's place had felt as much like home to her as the family ranch in Texas.

"I'm sorry that douchebag didn't treat you right. Rich guys think they can act like idiots and get away with it. But I gotta tell ya, breaking you out like that…well, that shit was fun." The driver grinned.

Mercy flashed him a *shit happens* grimace, while inside she was dying. Each block melted into the next until the distance from Kellan's house made her feel as if she were traveling to some other planet in the solar system. The driver continued talking, but she blocked him out. She was too wrapped up in the unrelenting arms of hurt and anger.

She wondered what Kellan would do once he found her gone. Would he be pissed that she'd left…forced an end to his game? Or would he eagerly begin seeking out his next victim? Did anyone at Club Genesis know he was married? No. They wouldn't condone that type of behavior…would they? Was cheating on your spouse accepted in the community?

It doesn't matter since you won't be going back to the club…ever!

Unfortunately, she would have to return, at least to talk to Mika. After all, she had to retrieve her car and tell him to cancel her membership.

She closed her eyes and exhaled in defeat.

Suddenly a light bulb went off in her brain. She could find a quiet booth in the back of Maurizio's—the Italian restaurant not far from the club where members liked to meet up and enjoy dinner before play—and simply wait for Mika to arrive. Showing her face to a handful of members versus a whole dungeon was easier to swallow. The chance of running into Kellan at the restaurant was fifty-fifty—the chance of seeing him at the club…one hundred percent.

Maurizio's it is.

Directing the driver to her building, Mercy paid her fare and extracted her key. The man chivalrously carried her belongings inside and left them next to her apartment door.

"Thank you for all your help. You've been a lifesaver."

"You're welcome. So…what's your answer?"

"To what?"

"You know...what I asked you about in the car...you and me. I'd treat you tons better than that rich prick."

"Oh." She blanched wishing she'd paid more attention. "Uh, well...you're offer is sweet, really, but I need a break from relationships for a while."

"I get it. Yeah, I'm not interested in being a rebound guy. But..." He fished a business card out of his pocket and shot her a seductive smile. "If you need any help licking your wounds, give me a call."

Startled by his innuendo, Mercy was even more stunned when the guy quickly kissed her on the cheek, then turned and walked out the lobby door.

Ewww! One stalker is more than enough, thank you!

Standing in the open, alone, she felt as if someone was watching her. An uneasy chill spread through her, and Mercy quickly unlocked her door. She glanced at the sidelight windows flanking the main door but didn't see anyone. Shaking off her paranoia, she shoved her belongings past the portal and flipped on the lights. Mercy half expected to see another ghastly message splashed across her walls, but thankfully, the fresh smell of paint was the only unusual thing to greet her. She quickly closed and locked the door behind her, then dealt with unpacking. Mercy figured the fewer memories of Kellan staring her in the face, the better.

She toted the duffel bag to her bedroom and sighed when she saw the bare mattress. After drawing out a set of clean sheets and several blankets from the linen closet, Mercy made the bed and unpacked her clothes.

When her chores were done, she donned her favorite flannel pajamas. She then poured a glass of wine, set her phone on the docking station, and turned on some mellow music. Sitting on the couch with her feet tucked beneath her, Mercy stared at the dark splintered television screen.

"That thing looks just like my heart...a broken, fractured web of nothing." The words rolled off her tongue in a humorless scoff. "I still can't believe the bastard's married. What. The. Fuck?"

Mercy drained the merlot in two gulps. Twirling the stem between her fingers and thumb, she stared at the circling rim. Memories of the night Kellan taught her how to kneel and serve him danced in her head. She could still taste the wine's fruity flavor exploding over her tongue as he shared the first sip with her.

A tear slid down her cheek.

Mercy absently brushed it away.

CHAPTER NINE

KELLAN ANXIOUSLY PUNCHED in the code, cursing the lost seconds before the annoying buzzer sounded. He yanked the door open and sprinted down the hall, ignoring everyone and everything around him.

Please, God. Don't let me be too late. He sent up a silent prayer as he darted into the room.

"You rest easy, Miss Leena. Your man is on his way to see you," Lucia murmured softly as she stroked his wife's hair.

No longer sitting up to stare at the wall, Leena lay on the bed, eyes closed as if sleeping. The left side of her mouth sagged in a deep frown, while the other side seemingly now lifted in a semi-peaceful smile.

Tears burned in his eyes.

A lump of emotion swelled in his throat.

His feet felt like cement.

And guilt continued to eat him alive.

If Kellan had been with Natalie when he'd received the frightening call, he could have easily compartmentalized his shame...locked it away in a cold and meaningless vault. But he had been with Mercy. His feelings for her were far from meaningless, and Kellan had carelessly given in to that love.

You knew...you fucking knew! his subconscious railed.

Yes, he *had* known...known the first time he laid eyes on Mercy, that his orderly, disciplined life would eventually go up in smoke. Still, Kellan had foolishly continued reinforcing the walls of his heart, hoping to maintain his restraint and distance. But as he watched her at the club, dreamed about her night after night, the ache to guide her to her knees and claim her fucking soul had annihilated his almighty control.

Mercy owned *him*, and there wasn't a fucking thing Kellan could do to change that fact.

"Oh, Mr. Graham," Lucia's tone dripped with sorrow.

"What happened?" He forced the words past his lips.

"An hour ago, her blood pressure began to spike. Poor thing started to seize. Dr. Weaver gave her an injection to break down the blood clots, but…"

Kellan nodded trying not to fixate on the image of Leena having another seizure. He'd already witnessed three over the past five years. He knew, from previous diagnoses, the unstable synapses in her brain could easily trigger strokes, but this one was by far the worst Leena had endured.

"Go on and tend to your other patients, Lucia. I'll stay with her."

"All right, but you ring me right away if you notice any changes in our girl."

"I will." He forced a smile.

Kellan took Leena's hand and stared at her while remorse shredded his soul. He wanted to crawl in bed with her, hold her in his arms. Instead, he sat beside her and started to confess his sins.

When he was done, tears stained his cheeks. His temples throbbed as he wiped his nose and exhaled a heavy sigh.

"I'm sorry, baby. I love you…I'll always love you, but I'm so fucking empty inside. She fills me up, the way you used to. I know…I know. I'm being a selfish prick, but goddammit, I've locked myself away all these years, just like you." He sniffed. "I keep thinking…what if our roles were reversed? God, Leena, I wouldn't want you to stop living. The love inside you…fuck…it's vast and beautiful. I'd never want you to let it wither away because of me."

"She wouldn't. Leena wouldn't want yours to wither away because of her either." Mika moved in behind him and gripped Kellan's shoulder. "Hannah called me. She's on her way."

"Thanks for coming, man." Kellan sniffed and wiped his eyes.

Mika stared at Leena for several silent minutes. "This is the hardest thing life will ever throw your way, brother. I know you don't think so…especially now, but you will survive it."

"I know," Kellan answered lowly. "Every time I think I can't take another day of this…the pain you went through with Vanessa comes crashing in my head."

"I'm not inviting you to drink the grape Kool-Aid or anything, but I need to tell you something. I haven't talked about this with anyone other than Julianna and my dad. The night that Dennis McCollum shot me, I died. Flat lined…lights out…end of the road. But before the EMTs revived me and brought me back…" Mika scrubbed a hand over his bald head. "I went someplace…someplace beyond this earth. My mom and Vanessa were there. They told me things that changed the way I thought about life. Their…*insight,* I guess you'd call it, gave me the courage to let Julianna inside my heart."

Kellan silently listened, studying his friend. Mika wasn't filling him full of hopeful clichés about life and death, but relaying firsthand experience and the lessons he'd learned.

"I was fighting my feelings for Julianna and Dad was fighting his for Sarah. Mom and Vanessa were pissed that we were both too hardheaded to let the women they sent us into our hearts. The people who love us…well, all they want is for us to be happy. That's what I want for you, too, brother."

Kellan stood. He wrapped Mika in a manly hug and clapped him on the back.

"Thank you for sharing that with me. It means…a lot."

"Don't let guilt eat you alive. I've been there, done that, and wasted a lot of precious time." Mika sent him a sympathetic look. "I'm going to head out. Just wanted to stop by and let you know I'm here for you. If you need anything, give me a call."

"I will." Kellan nodded soberly.

"Is Mercy…"

"She's still at my place. Shit! I flew out of the house in such a rush I'm not even sure what I said to her." Kellan pinched the bridge of his nose in an attempt to ease his pounding head.

"When you touch base with her, give her my number and tell her to call if she needs anything, all right?"

"Will do. Thanks again. You being here is a huge help."

"I'll be back again to see you soon, sweet girl." Mika leaned over the bed and brushed a kiss on Leena's forehead. He turned and a ghost of a smile kicked up a corner of his mouth. "In reality, we're fucking lucky. We get to carry the love of two incredible women in our hearts every day. Lucky bastards, for sure."

Mika left and Kellan sat by Leena's side, talking to her about life and love and the happy times they shared. A short time later, Hannah ran into the room, her pale face blotched in red as tears poured down her cheeks. Kellan scooped up his grown-up little girl and placed her on his lap. Hannah curled up against him as she'd done as a child and let him hold her as she cried. Sometimes age and independence took a backseat to the soothing unconditional love of a parent.

Kellan watched the skies lighten as dawn began to break. Hannah slept with her head resting on Leena's bed, holding her mother's hand. There had been no change in his wife's condition throughout the night. He wanted to breathe a sigh of relief but knew she wasn't out of the woods yet. Even with the anticoagulant injections, there were no guarantees her damaged brain would withstand yet another stroke. It was the same slow, agonizing waiting game that Kellan had been forced to play before.

When Hannah woke, he sent her to the cafeteria to get some breakfast. She returned a half an hour later and shooed him out the door to eat as well. As he drew closer to the dining hall, the scent of food made him nauseous. He continued walking and he pulled out his phone.

Mercy didn't pick up and his call went to her voice mail. A tiny smile tugged his lips. The punishment he'd handed down yesterday had left the impression he'd wanted. Still, he hadn't come home last night and wanted to alleviate any anxiety or worry. He thought about calling Mika to drop by and check on her, but Hannah's frantic cry from the opposite end of the hall had Kellan sprinting toward his daughter instead.

Darting back into the room with his heart in his throat, he watched Leena's chest rise and fall and exhaled a heavy breath.

"She squeezed my hand," Hannah sobbed joyfully. "Mom...just squeezed my hand."

Kellan held his daughter and closed his eyes. Yes, Leena had squeezed his hand once before as well. He now had to dash his daughter's hope, as Dr. Weaver had done to Kellan's, and explain that it was nothing more than a spontaneous muscle twitch. Of course, Hannah didn't want to believe him—hell, he hadn't wanted to believe the doctor, either—but Kellan managed to talk his daughter off the ledge. Cursing this heartbreaking hand life had dealt them all, he held her once more as Hannah fell apart.

By afternoon, the city was blanketed with a light snow. Kellan had tried to raise Mercy several times, but she still did not answer. Anxious and edgy, he paced Leena's room, then the halls. His restlessness only increased.

"You're driving me nuts, Daddy. Go home and check on her. I'll stay with Mom, okay?"

He was torn between the love he'd lost and the new love he'd found, and the indecision warring within was maddening. Kellan wasn't the wavering type, yet there he stood, vacillating and unsure.

"I might be awhile, sweetheart. I need to explain…I don't know if she'll even understand all this."

"You won't until you try."

"Sometimes you're smart beyond your years, you know it?"

"I had very good teachers." She sent him a bittersweet smile. "Go."

Kellan returned to the house, entering from the garage into the kitchen. The ropes he'd used to tie Mercy lay on the floor. A rush of comfort…familiarity coursed through his veins, followed by confusion when he noticed her computer, cell phone and MP3 player were no longer on the table.

Why would she put her things away but leave the rope on the floor?

"Mercy!" he shouted, listening intently for her reply.

When none came, he bounded up the stairs, two at a time, telling himself that she was taking a nap. He rounded the doorway of the guest room, but Mercy wasn't there. The dresser drawers were open and empty. So was the closet. Turning, he saw the lamp, or what was left of it, smashed to pieces on the floor.

She was gone. Packed her things and left.

Kellan sucked in a deep breath and expelled a mighty roar.

He'd been so stunned and panicked when Lucia had called, he couldn't remember what he'd said to Mercy. He closed his eyes and struggled to recall his movements…and more importantly, his words.

"Wait here. I'll be back…I-I'm not sure when. But I'll be back."

"Is something wrong? Kellan, you're scaring me. Is it Hannah? Is she sick? Has she been in an accident?"

"No! It's my wife."

"Fuck!"

As he had done hours before, Kellan turned and ran down the stairs and into the garage. This time he wasn't speeding toward the nursing home fearing what he would find…this time he was racing toward Mercy's apartment with the same gut-churning dread. Driving too fast on the slushy roads, he skidded through a stop sign and kept going. Working to keep his car on the road, Kellan struggled to align the words he wanted to say to Mercy. He knew he might have but one chance to make things right. He wasn't going to fuck it up.

He pulled into a parking space near her complex door and nearly landed on his ass exiting the car. With a muttered curse, he hurried into the foyer and raised his hand before pounding on her door.

"Mercy, open up. We need to talk."

"It's a little too late for that, Your Honor," she scoffed from the other side of the portal.

"Look, I know you're mad—"

"Oh, I'm not mad, Kellan." *Liar*, he thought at the icy tone of her voice. "I'm quite fine, actually. Please leave and don't come back."

"You know that's not going to happen…not until we talk."

"Talk all you want…to the door. I'm going to take a shower. Bye-bye."

Her smartassed dismissal burned like acid.

Break the fucking door down, the angry beast inside encouraged.

No. Kerr had inflicted enough damage to her pride and property. Kellan wasn't going to destroy any more of her than he probably already had. Shoving his hands in his pockets, he dropped his chin and exhaled as he pondered the best way to reach a plausible compromise so she would at least unlock the fucking door.

He slid the ring of his keychain between his finger and thumb as a slow, evil smile drew across his lips.

"Mercy. Open the door, angel."

"Go away, Kellan, or I swear I'll call the damn cops."

Going to take a shower, huh? No. She was probably peering at him though the peephole, watching his every move.

"Don't make me repeat myself, girl. You know what will happen."

"Yeah. I do. Not a goddamn thing. You don't have a say in what I do anymore, mister. So fuck off!"

Oh, yeah…she's not mad at all. Bullshit!

"Fuck off, huh," he stated, lifting the spare key to her apartment in front of the tiny glass circle of the door.

"Don't you dare! This is *my* apartment and that's *my* key. Put it under the mat and leave!"

Though technically it wasn't breaking and entering...after all, he did have a key, Mercy could file charges against him that even *he* wouldn't be able to wriggle out of.

A newspaper headline flashed in his head: CIRCUIT COUNTY JUDGE KELLAN GRAHAM ARRESTED!

Was forcing Mercy to talk to him worth potentially ending his career?

Yes! Hands down!

"Sorry, angel," he softly replied. Sliding the key into the lock, he turned the metal. "I can't do that."

He tried to open the door, but Mercy had her petite frame pressed up against it. Though he didn't want to hurt her, Kellan lowered his shoulder against the wood and shoved his way inside.

She stumbled back, mouth agape, eyes rimmed red, then let out an ear-piercing scream. "You bastard! Get the fuck out of my apartment."

Before he could open his mouth to speak, Mercy grabbed a heavy-looking statue off the console table beside the door. Kellan dropped his keys and grabbed her wrist before she could knock him the fuck out.

"Take your hands off me," she spat.

Fire blazed in her eyes, but there was a world of hurt mixed with her fury that damn near took him out at the knees. He'd put it there. Made her think he was nothing but a low-life cheating sleazeball. In a way, he was, and Kellan knew then that words weren't going to be enough. He glanced down at her feet.

"Good. You're wearing shoes. Get a coat. I need you to come with me."

"In your dreams," she hissed. "I'm not going anywhere with you. Why are you even here? Your little game is over, asshole! Go home to your *wife*!"

Exhausted. Stressed. Pissed as a lion with a sore paw, Kellan's patience had reached its limit.

"Get your coat, or I'll toss you over my shoulder and haul you out to my car without one."

"You touch me and I'll slap you with assault so fast it'll make your head spin," she countered angrily.

"Go ahead," he shrugged. Fast as lightning, he plucked her off the ground and tossed her over his shoulder.

Mercy yelped and kicked as she pummeled his back with her fists. He felt as if he were trying to contain a Tasmanian devil.

"Don't say I didn't warn you."

"Put me down. Goddammit, Kellan put me down. I'll get my fucking coat."

"I don't believe you, sweetheart. See, I think the minute I put you down, you're going to try and either kick me in the balls or run to the kitchen and draw a knife on me."

"Argh!" she growled.

"That's why you're going to stop screaming, kicking, and fighting and let me carry you out to my car."

"In case you didn't get the memo, I am *not* your submissive."

"Oh, I figured you'd taken back your control when you told me to fuck off."

"Wrong. I took it back the second you told me you had a *wife*!"

"Fair enough…for now."

"Where is it you've got such a hard-on to take me, anyway?" She asked. "I'm not going back to your house, so you can forget that."

"I'm not taking you there." He couldn't mask the sorrow in his voice.

"Kellan? Please put me down. What's happened? What's going on?"

Her combative tone had vanished, replaced with worry and concern. Hoping he wasn't making a huge mistake, Kellan bent and set Mercy back on her feet.

"It's not good. It's something I should have talked to you about days ago, but I-I couldn't bring myself to tell you…"

"Tell me what?"

"No, love. It's better if I just show you."

KELLAN'S CRYPTIC REPLY confused her, but it was the pain in his eyes that pierced her heart. No matter how badly she wanted to refuse him, turn him away, and block him from her life…she couldn't.

She loved him.

"I'll get my coat."

A million questions rolled through her mind as Kellan silently pulled out of her complex. The snow was falling harder now. Wet and heavy, it clung to the trees. She was glad for the heat blasting from the vent above her feet and the warmth of her own coat. Mercy paid attention to the street signs as he slowly maneuvered the slick roads.

Several blocks later, Kellan pulled in to the parking lot of Lake Home Village Nursing and Assisted Living Center. She shot him a quizzical look, but he simply turned off the ignition and took her hand.

"We need to go inside."

She didn't reply, simply nodded at his staid expression. Mercy stood beside him as he punched in a code for the front door. A loud buzz sounded and he pulled the handle, allowing her to enter first. As he followed in behind her, she caught sight of several elderly people slowly walking the halls. Some leaned on their walkers as they smiled and talked. Some waved to Kellan sadly. He acknowledged their greeting with a nod of his head, then gently slid a palm to Mercy's back and led her down a long hallway.

She felt a spiritless pall rolling off Kellan and wondered if his father-in-law or maybe mother-in-law lay in one of the rooms, possibly dying. His anguish was palpable. Its weight pressed in around her. She wanted to ease his pain but didn't know how.

When he stopped at the doorway of the last room, Hannah stood, eyes rimmed red, wearing a trembling smile.

"I saw you pull in. I'm going to go sit in the lobby and give you two some privacy."

"Thank you, sweetheart." He kissed his daughter's cheek.

Hannah hugged Mercy and whispered in her ear, "Try to keep an open mind. Daddy needs you." Then she turned and walked away.

"Step inside, please." The devastation etched in his face filled her with shame for lashing out at him and trying to turn him away.

With a nervous nod, she walked beside him and into the room.

Tears filled her eyes as she gazed upon the once vibrant woman she'd seen in the photo in Kellan's room.

"This is my wife, Leena. I know I should have told you about her before now, but..." He turned and drilled Mercy with an almost pleading stare. "I was afraid. Afraid that you'd tell me to...well, to fuck off, and you did. I'm not a misogynistic prick who fucks around on his wife. I love her...love her very much. I always have and always will. We shared an amazing life together." His voice cracked.

He paused and stared down at his wife. A bittersweet smile graced his lips.

"The phone call yesterday... Leena suffered a stroke." Kellan settled his gaze on Mercy once more. "I'm sorry I didn't explain the situation before I lost control, and... I'll take you back home."

Mercy's heart ached for Kellan and the guilt he was obviously struggling with. She gazed back at Leena, remembering the happy glow of her face in the photo...the depth of love they'd shared. The jealousy Mercy had embraced was gone, replaced by a feeling of loss and sadness that broke her heart all over again. Not for herself but for Kellan and Hannah.

Numbly, she let him lead her out of the room and back down the long hallway. Kellan stepped away and spoke to Hannah briefly, then escorted Mercy out the front door. An awkward silence hung in the air as he drove. She stared out the window as a million questions swirled through her mind, like the fat, heavy snowflakes that were floating to the ground.

When they reached her apartment, Kellan walked Mercy inside.

"Would you like to come in? I can make some coffee."

"Coffee would be nice. Thanks."

Mercy shucked off her coat and hurried to the kitchen. As she filled the coffeemaker, she watched Kellan glance around the family room.

"I haven't had time to check with Amblin today, to see if they've picked up Kerr. Please be careful and..." His voice cracked again.

Mercy watched as tears filled Kellan's eyes. She rushed to him and wrapped her arms around him.

"I'm truly sorry. Sorry for everything. I should have been stronger and held on to the discipline I've been clinging to for the past five years. But...every night at the club I spent watching you, I let you crawl a little deeper inside me. Dammit. I didn't just break my own rules, I broke every Dominant rule with you as well. I wasn't honest. Didn't communicate. I failed you on every level, angel. I'm sorry for that as well."

"Stop. You don't have to apologize."

"Yes. I do. I've made a mess of things. I had no right to touch you. The past few days I've spent with you have made me feel alive. *You* brought me back to life." He pulled away, cupped Mercy's cheek, and gazed into her eyes. "Being with you has made me want to start living again. Yes, I'm married, but Hannah was right, it is time for me to go on. To make a new life…new memories. Though I'd never ask you to throw away your morals or change your beliefs—God knows I've spent years struggling with that myself—I've fallen in love with you, angel. I want to build a new life…with you."

The ground beneath her feet began to crumble.

Tears spilled down her cheeks.

Mercy covered her mouth to hold back a sob.

Kellan pulled her against him tighter, and she could feel him trembling. "I'm sorry I brought you into this mess, but I'm not sorry for loving you."

His voice was thick with emotion.

The aloof and elusive Master was gone. In his place was a man…a mortal man with fears and flaws and all things human. He'd shed his protective walls and allowed her to see his weaknesses. Still, Kellan's potent Dominant command—the same demeanor that had drawn her to him from the start—wrapped her in warmth and surety.

"I love you, too," she confessed in a whisper.

KELLAN SAT WITH one arm extended, clutching his dying wife's hand, and holding his weeping daughter with the other. Leena had suffered several minor strokes over the past five days, but Dr. Weaver sadly revealed the one that assaulted her hours ago would claim her from this earth.

"You'll always be in our hearts, baby," Kellan choked out as her breathing slowed. Tears flowed down his face. "I love you, Leena."

When she stopped breathing, Hannah cried out in anguish. She buried her head in Leena's lap and sobbed.

"Good-bye, my love," he whispered.

Kellan kissed his wife's cheek for the last time, then gathered Hannah into his arms.

They held each other and cried for a long, long time.

While he and Hannah sat at Leena's side, waiting for the director of the funeral home to arrive, memories marched through Kellan's mind.

Though racked with grief, he found solace reliving the happy times that had brightened his world. The love he'd shared with Leena was as unique as the growing love between him and Mercy. Both women were intriguing, rare, full of sass and humor and fiery passion. Kellan was a lucky man to be sure.

He'd come to terms with the guilt of living and loving again; saying good-bye before they wheeled Leena away was hell.

Kellan dried his eyes and led his crying daughter out of the nursing home. He held her hand as they drove back to his house though the gently falling snow.

When he and Hannah stepped inside the kitchen, Mercy met them at the door. Tears streamed down her cheeks and she wrapped Hannah in a warm embrace. Mercy turned her glistening aqua eyes up at him, silently asking if he was okay. Kellan nodded and placed a gentle kiss on her forehead.

"There's hot stew on the stove and fresh coffee in the pot."

"I think I need something stronger than coffee," Kellan replied.

"McClellan," Hannah sniffed. "Make it a double."

After drinks and stew, they spent the rest of the afternoon sitting by the fire while he and Hannah reminisced, telling stories about Leena. At first, he worried Mercy would be uncomfortable with the funny and melancholy memories, but she laughed and cried right along with them.

Hang on to her. She's one in a million.

Startled at the sound of Leena's voice inside his head, Kellan swallowed tightly as tears stung his eyes. *I will, my love.*

The following Saturday, surrounded by more than a hundred friends, with Hannah and Mercy at his side, Kellan buried his wife. He'd known for five long, agonizing years this day would come, but he hadn't fully prepared for the emotional impact.

It was the hardest and saddest day of his life.

Kellan sat on the couch, sipping a glass of scotch, absorbed in his own thoughts.

Finality.

The word circled through his head. He'd not only buried his wife but had found a private moment to terminate his contract with Natalie.

Kellan had found the respite and fire he'd barred from his life right beside him.

Mercy silently curled up against his chest. Without a second thought, she'd extended her love, support, and understanding over these past heartbreaking and tumultuous days.

Kellan was finally at peace with himself.

It was time to give back to her.

"Go upstairs and draw us a hot bath in the whirlpool, angel."

She sent him a smile, then kissed him softly. "I know you didn't give me permission, but I couldn't help myself."

Kellan gazed into her eyes, feeling a different kind of warmth seeping into his system. He gripped her waist and dragged her onto his lap. Cupping her nape, he pulled her to his lips and kissed her hard. The heat of her body surrounded him. He let the warmth of her love melt his sorrow.

Straddling him, she ground her pussy against his erection and grinned. "We may not make it all the way upstairs."

"Maybe not, but we'll definitely be making something…making love."

He kissed her, sliding his tongue into her silky mouth, and then cupped his hands beneath the cheeks of her ass. As he stood, he lifted her with him, never breaking the kiss that had grown raw and passionate. Mercy wrapped her legs around his waist as Kellan carried her up the stairs.

Anticipation mounted, sizzling and crackling in the air around them.

While he'd spent his days and most of his nights by Leena's side, Mika and the Genesis gang had moved Mercy into Kellan's house. The nights he did return home, he was too emotionally spent to do anything but gather her into his arms and fall asleep.

His past was now gone…buried in a patch of ground near a sprawling oak tree.

It was time for Kellan to start a new life…here and now.

He grinned against Mercy's lips as she clung to him like a crab while he crawled onto the middle of the bed.

She pulled from his lips and narrowed her eyes. "What's so funny?"

"You," he teased before turning decidedly sober. "Thank you for…being you, Mercy."

"You don't have to thank me for anything…I love you."

"I love you, and I aim to show you just how much, too."

"Not if I show you first." The mischievous grin tugging her lips melted his heart.

Reaching between her head and the pillow, Kellan fisted her hair and gave a little tug.

A flare of hunger flashed in her eyes. Her pupils widened.

Mine!

"Who's in charge, girl?"

With a coy smile, she softly moaned. "You, Sir…always."

CHAPTER TEN

MERCY HAD WAITED what felt like a lifetime for Kellan to hover over her like this…like her fantasies. But was he emotionally ready to make love to her? The sliver of worry that Kellan was moving too fast zipped through her head.

After he'd revealed that he loved her, he'd explained what had happened to his wife…the hopes and dreams they'd had. Mercy assured him she had no qualms loving a married man. Some might view her a whore, but she didn't care. No one could call her a home wrecker; the drunk who'd run Leena down held that title.

Kellan worried Mercy would think him an adulterer. Of course, she *had* thought that very thing, at least until she'd learned the truth. It broke her heart that he'd locked himself away inside a self-imposed prison for five long years. Still, she'd almost turned him down when he invited her to move in with him, but if they were going to survive in any aspect—be it friends or lovers—she had to trust him.

Mercy let him set the pace those few short days ago; she'd trust his decision now.

She closed her eyes as Kellan brushed his lips along her jaw, down her throat, nipping her flesh as he worked his way to the sensitive spot behind her ear. Tingles turned to goose bumps that peppered her arms. A whimper seeped from her lips while the ache between her legs grew and soaked her panties.

After slowly peeling off her clothes, Kellan dragged the pads of his fingers over her skin. His touch ignited that familiar warmth, the awakening of the man who owned her heart, sank into her soul. His masterful fingers circled the crinkled flesh of her areolas like a blind man reading braille. Lifting, she arched, scraping her stiff peaks against his palms.

Gliding his tongue down her neck, he pressed it flat against the pulse point. "Your heart is racing, angel. Are you excited about all the wicked things I'm going to do to you?" His voice was sinfully deep and whiskey smooth.

"Yes," she answered breathlessly. "Please, show me."

"I'll do more than show you. I'm going to draw every ounce of pleasure from your wicked body, over and over."

Kellan flicked his tongue at her taut nipple. Mercy gasped and softly raked her nails across his back. Unrelenting, he feasted on her breasts, one after the other, until her swollen peaks grew tender. Each scrape of his teeth followed by the swirling lave of his tongue melded the shards of pain into blissful pleasure.

He commanded her body, but not for his own sadistic pleasure. Even when he scraped his teeth over her inflamed nipples, Kellan heightened the pleasure with a blissful sweep of his tongue…melding the two opposing sensations in spine-bending harmony.

The torture was exquisite.

"Your skin tastes sweet…addicting." His voice was a raspy murmur.

A trail of fire ignited her flesh as Kellan skimmed his lips and tongue down her body.

Anticipation multiplied as Mercy lay trembling in complete surrender.

Inching lower still, he nipped the thin skin covering her pelvic bones. Her pussy clutched at the strange erotic sensation. She rolled her hips, unable to contain her mounting need or the moan that slid off her tongue when he settled his warm hand over her bare mound.

Her swollen clit throbbed in time with her pounding heart. Mercy ached for his thick fingers to part her folds and slide deep inside her weeping core.

Kellan had other plans.

Raking a hungry gaze down her body, he lightly slapped the fleshy bow between her legs. The vibration teased her needy clit.

"Oh, god," Mercy moaned.

He replied by increasing the tempo and strength of each swat. Burning heat enveloped her flesh and Mercy slightly parted her thighs.

"That's it, angel. Yes…wider for me," he encouraged. "Wide so I can see your pretty wet folds."

Bending her knees, she spread her legs.

Kellan dragged his fingers through her dripping folds and then landed a wet slap atop her mound. A surge of pain spread up her stomach and down her pussy, rolling beneath her skin to meld and coil at her clit. She stretched her legs so wide the insides of her thighs grew taut.

"That's it, little one. Proudly show me what's mine. I enjoy inspecting every slick pink fold…the ripples and ridges inside my sinfully beautiful cunt."

"Kellan," she whimpered.

He landed a quick but brutal wet slap across her pussy. Mercy let out a howl and immediately started to close her legs.

"No!" Kellan gripped her thighs and spread her open once more. "How do you address me?"

"Sir," she gasped, riding the blistering wave cresting through her.

"I think it's time we move past Sir, now. Don't you? Call me Master, angel."

"Yes, Master," she replied with a quiver of delight.

The teacher had now become the Master…her Master, claiming her as his own.

Tears of happiness slid from her eyes.

"Good girl," he praised low and lovingly.

Supporting himself on his elbows, Kellan stretched onto his stomach and began tracing his finger along the outline of her swollen, wet folds. Mercy mewled. Her hungry core clutched the empty air.

"Yes, just like I'd dreamed. Your cunt's ripe like a peach." He leaned in close and inhaled a deep breath. "Mmm, smells sweet like one, too."

He smiled up at her and extended his tongue. Mercy watched, whimpered, and quivered as he slowly dragged it up her center. His chin glistened and he closed his eyes and moaned.

"Much better than a peach," he growled. "Juicier. Sweeter. Oh, yes, angel, you taste much, much better."

He gave her no warning before he lunged his mouth over her cunt. Lapping, sucking, scraping, he devoured her with his teeth and tongue. Kellan soon added his fingers into play, driving deep inside her as he suckled her clit. The roar of release thundered in her ears, but Mercy knew she couldn't let go, couldn't fragment into that explosive bliss without permission. A permission she feared was light-years from rolling off his tongue.

With his lips wrapped around her clit, he batted his tongue back and forth over the sensitive nub. The room was spinning, or maybe it was her mind, but soon she was going to go down in flames.

She sank her fingers into his thick, dark hair and held on for dear life.

But when he began spreading her hot cream over the puckered rim of her ass, sparks of lightning shot through her and she clutched his scalp.

"Oh, please…no," she cried. "No. I can't hold back if you do that…please, Master. Don't."

Kellan lifted from her clit and sent her a wicked smile as he pressed the tip of his finger through her gathered rim.

Mercy rocked her hips. Taking his digit deeper, she let out a lusty moan.

"Oh, angel. I'm going to love tormenting your tight little ass." To emphasize his words, Kellan wiggled his finger as she tightened around him. "But I'm going to love fucking your sinful little hole, claiming you here a whole lot more."

"Master!"

"I am…and I'm never going to let you forget it."

The love and promise in his eyes melted her heart.

Without another word, Kellan dipped his head and began devouring her once more.

The lash of his tongue, the thrust of his fingers filling and stretching her was too much. She dangled at the edge of release by sheer will alone. Her body and mind fused, and Mercy's keening cries echoed all around her as she melted beneath his salacious assault.

"Come for me, angel. Come hard!" Kellan bellowed.

He shoved his fingers deep and sucked her clit between his lips.

"Master!" she cried as the thunder consumed her.

Lights flashed behind her eyes.

Her muscles gripped tight around him. Mercy bore down beneath the weight of release.

"Jesus," he hissed as she seized his fingers.

Blinded in bliss, Mercy shattered.

Kellan continued to thrust through her clutching tunnels, riding the waves of ecstasy with her as she screamed and writhed. Slowly, he brought her back down and eased from inside her. He crawled up the bed and gathered her boneless sated body into his arms.

Mercy felt his rigid, throbbing cock pressed against her thigh and whimpered.

She lifted her leg and shifted her weight until her folds enveloped the length of his heated shaft.

Kellan groaned and claimed her in a raw and urgent kiss.

Mercy ached to rise up and slide onto his cock. To feel him fill and stretch her as she rode him to the same oblivion he'd granted her.

"I need a condom." His voice was tight, strained.

"I'm on the pill. I'm clean," she explained breathlessly before kissing him again.

Mercy could taste herself as Kellan plunged his tongue into her mouth. He gripped her hips and lifted her off his pulsating erection. As he aligned the crest to her cunt, she clutched and softly kissed his wide, wet tip.

With a feral roar, he pulled down on her hips as he thrust all the way inside her. She tore from his mouth and cried out beneath a sublime and wicked burn that consumed her core.

"So tight. So hot…"

"Yes. Oh, god…yes," she panted.

Kellan drew her against his chest and rolled, pinning her beneath him. He pulled back and dragged his cock through her fiery passage. Mercy wiggled, working to relax her muscles.

"Am I hurting you?"

"Yes, but it's divine agony," she mewled.

"Will you suffer for me?"

If this was his idea of suffering, she'd gladly take all the agony he'd give.

"Always, Master."

"Arms above your head, slave."

His declaration that she was his *slave* filled her with joy and pride.

All Mercy's dreams had come true.

She raised her arms and gripped the base of the headboard, then stared up at him.

Love flowed from his deep blue eyes and surged into her veins.

"Use me, Master…use me to fulfill all your needs," she whispered softly.

Kellan cursed beneath his breath. Bending low, he kissed her as he dragged his thick cock in and out of her snug core. He strummed her sore nipples with a featherlight touch, then laved and kissed the peaks, all the while thrusting in and out, teasing the tightly knit bundle of nerves deep inside her.

Like a conductor, he played her body, heart, and soul masterfully, building her senses to a blinding, beautiful crescendo, only to thwart her with a demand not to come. Mercy fought every primal urge inside her to stave off her release.

For a brief moment, she wondered if he would leave her suspended and suffering for infinity. But as she watched pleasure and determination play over his face, she knew his almighty control was crumbling as rapidly as hers.

Sweat dripped from his brow; his labored breaths mirrored her own. As he shuttled in and out of her, the friction of his passion and demand blazed her insides like fire. His shaft swelled impossibly larger, lighting up her G-spot and sending pulses of lightning to numb her limbs.

She was going to come. Even the fear of failing him couldn't keep her from holding back to the tide within.

"Help me! Master…" Her plea-stained cry reverberated in her ears.

He gripped her hips and buried his cock to the hilt. Staring down at her with such unconditional love and devotion she wanted to cry, he jerked his head.

"Come!" Kellan bellowed.

They sailed to the heavens united in the blinding light of love and shattered into a million shards of ecstasy…together.

KELLAN KICKED THE SNOW off his boots, hung the shovel on the hook in the garage, and stepped inside the kitchen. Mercy stood at the stove and raised her eyes to him.

"What?" he asked. Quickly glancing down, he saw the melting snow puddling on the floor. "I'll clean it up."

She laughed. "It's not that."

"Then what is it?"

"I used to hate the fact that every time I looked at you, my heart rate doubled and my pussy ached." She set the wooden spoon in her hand on the stove and sauntered his way with a bold, suggestive sway of her hips. "I don't mind it so much anymore."

He laughed and tugged her to his chest before wrapping his arms around her.

"Brrr." She shivered and tried to wriggle free. "Your coat…it's freezing cold."

He grinned and held on to her even tighter. "What's wrong? You don't like the cold?"

"I can't stand it. I'm from Texas, remember?"

"Why did you move to Chicago, then?"

"School…work…it sounded good at the time," she said with a shrug.

"I've got some chains in the dungeon. I could lay out in the snow for an hour or so, and then drape them over your—"

"What? I've been a perfect sub for weeks. I haven't tried to Top from the bottom. I've been working hard to learn all that you've been teaching me. Why are you talking about punishing me?"

"I wasn't. The icy chains aren't for punishment, angel…they're for fun…*my* fun."

Her eyes grew big. Her mouth opened and closed several times. It was all Kellan could do not to laugh.

"What's wrong, little one? Doesn't that sound like fun to you?"

"I think it sounds like the worst abusive torture on the planet…Sir."

"Then I guess you'd better continue being the *perfect sub*, huh?"

"Oh, I will." She swallowed tightly.

Kellan tugged her in close to his ear. "Not too perfect, angel. I kind of like your sassy attitude…within reason."

"That's good. Because it's not often I can bite my tongue."

"I've noticed," he drawled.

God, he loved teasing her.

Mercy rolled her eyes, then kissed him quickly before glancing at the growing puddle beneath his boots.

"Feel free to grab a towel and wipe that up," she quipped before heading back to the stove.

Kellan arched his brows, shucked off his coat and draped it over the hook by the door, then descended to the basement.

"Where are you going?" Mercy called down to him.

He didn't reply as he stepped into the dungeon and snagged a long length of chain. He rattled it noisily as he made his way back up the stairs. Watching the doorway, he wasn't disappointed when she appeared. Staring at the chains, a look of horror lined her face.

"I-I was only playing around with you, Master. I already wiped up the water. I was just j-joking. Honest."

Oh, yeah…keeping this little minx on her toes is going to be fun…a whole lot of fun.

Kellan reached the top of the stairs and brushed past her. Mercy followed on his heels, trying to backpedal her way out of trouble. Pausing at the door to the deck, he turned and coiled the chains in a tight circle.

"I think I'll leave those there for the time being, but watch yourself, angel. You never know when I might change my mind."

Mercy cocked her head and studied him intently. "You're messing with me on purpose, aren't you?"

He shrugged and shot her a wicked smile. "Want to find out?"

"No thank you."

Mercy quickly turned on her heel and scurried back to the kitchen.

Kellan stood in the family room and stared out at the ice covering the lake, then turned and watched Mercy stirring something on the stove. He made his way back to the kitchen and eased in behind her. Wrapping his arms around her waist, he buried his nose in her hair and inhaled the scent of soap and the citrusy lotion she used on her body.

"Smells delicious," he murmured in her ear.

Mercy tilted her head to one side, granting him access to the soft flesh of her neck. "It's a maple spicy mustard glaze for the pork roast I have in the oven."

"I'm talking about you." He lowered his voice, adding the edge of command that always captured her attention.

He smiled as he felt a shiver ripple through her.

"How much longer on the glaze?" he whispered dragging his tongue over the shell of her ear. Mercy moaned and stopped stirring. Purposely dragging his lips down the column of her neck, he knew she wouldn't answer. She never did when he drew her focus away in such a manner. Kellan stepped back and landed a harsh smack on her ass with his hand. "Answer me, slave."

"Five minutes." Her voice quivered.

"In seven minutes, I want you upstairs." He caressed the sting from her lush orbs with the palm of his hand. "Naked. On your knees with your luscious thighs spread nice and wide for me."

"Yes, Master," she replied in a breathless sigh.

As he left the kitchen and took the stairs to the second floor, Kellan could hear Mercy furiously tossing pots and pans behind him. A wide, satisfied smile spread across his lips as he yanked his sweater off over his head and stepped inside the bedroom.

Kellan passed the dresser and paused. A photo of him and Mercy, laughing at the Club Genesis Christmas party, now sat in a gilded frame where the photo of him and Leena once rested.

The conversation he and Mercy had had after Leena passed away came rushing back.

"I should go back to my apartment. I don't want to be in your way. You need time to mourn."

"Stay, please. I want and need you to stay. I started mourning the loss of my wife five years ago and stopped the day I met you. I can't lose you, too, Mercy. I love you."

"I'm not going anywhere, Kellan." She wrapped her arms around him and rested her head on his chest. "I thought all I ever craved was your command, but I know now…I crave you…all of you."

Kellan sucked in a deep breath, his chest expanded. From down the hall, he heard Mercy running his way. He had to bite back a laugh as she entered the bedroom, hopping on one leg as she yanked the knit yoga pants off the other. Finally freeing herself from her clothes, she slid to the floor, lowered her head—breathing heavily—and spread her legs with grace and flair. His cock instantly grew hard.

He silently circled her several times, drinking in her lush, heavy breasts, the straight line of her spine, and the sensual flare of her supple hips.

Mine!

Yes, she was his…in every way…heart, mind, body, and soul. Kellan was the luckiest bastard on the planet, and he damn well knew it.

"Are you hungry today, angel?" He stroked his hand over the top of her head, dragging his fingers through her hair.

"Famished, Master." She raised her head and flashed him a greedy stare.

"What is it that you're craving, my sweet slave?"

"You." A coy smile tugged her lips. "Your cock."

"My command?"

A flicker of delight danced in her eyes.

"Always, Master," she purred. "I'll always crave your command."

ABOUT THE AUTHOR

USA Today Bestselling author **Jenna Jacob** paints a canvas of passion, romance, and humor as her alpha men and the feisty women who love them unravel their souls, heal their scars, and find a happy-ever-after kind of love. Heart-tugging, captivating, and steamy, Jenna's books will surely leave you breathless and craving more.

A mom of four grown children, Jenna and her alpha-hunk husband live in Kansas. She loves reading, getting away from the city on the back of a Harley, music, camping, and cooking.

Meet her wild and wicked fictional family in Jenna's sultry series: ***The Doms of Genesis.*** Become spellbound by searing triple love connections in her continuing saga: ***The Doms of Her Life*** (co-written with the amazing Shayla Black and Isabella La Pearl). Journey with couples struggling to resolve their pasts and heal their scars to discover unbridled love and devotion in her contemporary series: ***Passionate Hearts.*** Or laugh along as Jenna lets her zany sense of humor and lack of filter run free in the romantic comedy series: ***Hotties of Haven.***

Connect with Jenna Online
Website: www.jennajacob.com
Email: jenna@jennajacob.com
Facebook Fan Page: facebook.com/authorjennajacob
Twitter: @jennajacob3
Instagram: instagram.com/jenna_jacob_author
Amazon Author Page: http://amzn.to/1GvwNnn
Newsletter: http://bit.ly/1Cj4ZyY

OTHER TITLES BY JENNA JACOB

The Doms of Genesis Series
Embracing My Submission
Masters of My Desire
Master of My Mind
Saving My Submission
Seduced By My Doms
Lured By My Master
Sin City Submission
Bound To Surrender
Resisting My Submission

The Doms of Her Life – Raine Falling Series
(Co-authored with Shayla Black and Isabella LaPearl)
One Dom To Love
The Young and The Submissive
The Bold and The Dominant
The Edge Of Dominance

The Passionate Hearts Series
Sky Of Dreams
Winds Of Desire (Coming Soon)

Hotties Of Haven Series
Sin On A Stick
Wet Dream
Revenge On The Rocks (Coming September 19, 2017)

Made in the USA
Middletown, DE
12 January 2018